I0775505

# Shadow of the Other Gods

## The Chronicles of Randy Carter Book 4

Sonya Lawson

SauceBox Press

# Contents

# Note to Reader

This book contains scenes that may depict, mention, or discuss: abduction, anxiety, assault, attempted murder, blood, death, kidnapping, murder, the occult, PTSD, queerphobia, and/or violence. Please take care of yourself as you read.

To the readers who've stuck with Randy and her crew. I can't thank you enough for taking a chance on an indie book that throws Lovecraft's characters and world upside down in so many ways. I couldn't have made it to this finish line without you.

# One

Baking metaphors were usually my jam, but things had been off lately. Mainly because my worldview went a little topsy-turvy. Made me think a little less about the calmness and joy of a life of baking and a little more about the history of the universe, or at least reality and our—or my—place in it.

This was the basic shape of reality I eventually learned, after a lot of lessons, some bullshit, and a smattering of trial and error in hazardous situations.

Before there was time and space, there was nothing—an unknowable void humans couldn't really fathom and probably didn't want to think about anyway. Then, chaos rolled and formed into being, ultimately calling itself into the shape of big old Daddy Azathoth. Next came the Outer Gods created by Azathoth, stretching and yawning in the unknown dark and given specific roles and titles and territories to look after or lord over. Then came stars, space, color, and sound... the breadth and depth of every universe and plane in existence stretching from the small little starting dot into eternity. Things like metal, dirt, water, and fire followed, all the building blocks of life in all worlds.

Next came the Elder Gods, then the Other Gods, maybe made with slight variation, except each was still made so they forever clawed and tore and destroyed in search of power and position. For the most part, at least. I had to believe at least a few of them were cool, for my own sanity.

Outer and Elder and Other Gods, being bored little shits, bore horrible, monstrous things. The humans came next. We came from chaos like everything else and were supposedly doomed to forever stumble in it without knowing all the shades and shapes lurking in the dark places we couldn't reach, much less understand. Unless a human was like me. Then they could learn enough to realize they don't know nearly enough—or learn enough to realize they should be very, very afraid of what was out there in the shadows and dark.

If they were extra lucky, like little old me, they'd learn enough to fight. To hurt others. To claw and grasp in their own way. I liked to think my shove toward the top of the food chain had been all about protection, but I guessed I wasn't not the one who could properly evaluate it. I lacked distance and have a clear bias. Whatever. I could say, in all honesty, I wanted to stick to a small world of baking, but swirling chaos had other plans for me. I was not expecting to save a whole slew of people I loved, and even some I didn't. How it all went down, and how I ended up falling headfirst into some weird-ass magic, was what was really important here.

THE FIRST FEW DAYS back from the Dreamlands were surreal, in good and bad ways. Because time and space was all wonky between the two worlds, we ended up back in Columbus the next day, our time. We had been gone from our world for a handful of hours, but it felt like way longer. In terms of what I learned about myself, what I had to go through, it might as well have been a lifetime.

The good: Mia was back. She wasn't exactly chipper or jumping for joy or anything, but she also didn't seem quite so haunted. She talked to us. She acted more open and not as secretive, even as the dark circles now seemed permanently etched under her eyes. There was also Rich, who'd hopped a ride back to Columbus with us. She'd gravitated toward him in a way I'd never seen her do with a dude before. For his part, he hovered around her, almost like she was the sun to his Earth, always circling. I couldn't really know if it was cool or not. Part of me wanted to bristle with big-sister energy and protectiveness, but I didn't. Mia was an adult. More than that, she was an adult who'd been through a boatload of trauma recently, so who was I to judge what made her feel okay? Still, I held on to my right to reserve judgment for a dude I guess was seeing my sister, although calling it "seeing" wasn't exactly right, given how they acted with one another.

Also of the good: Ny, Gareth, and I were all back and in one piece. Mostly. Ny was still without his Book of Knowing, thanks to Zeus running off before we could rip it away from him. He'd done a number on Ny when he'd taken over his Pharoah form, but my Outer God had held up well. He was his same sexy, powerful self after returning, though his time in the Dreamlands had given him more to think about beyond usual homecoming reflections.

Gareth was the "mostly" part of the mix. He'd held up well with all the Dreamlands craziness, including the pain he'd endured getting there and the gods he'd faced without blinking an eye. He'd also gotten a little piece of revenge, for himself, for his old friends, and for me and Mia when he took out Wilbur. The action, though, caused its own issues. Gareth had floated in nothingness for a few seconds, which was not long, except time was relative in weird spaces. There was a certain dullness to his hazel eyes and tension in his body I'd never seen before. He wouldn't discuss it, not right away. I'd give him time, but not the months I'd given Mia. I'd learned the hard way with that one. He'd have time and space to process on his own, but if needed, I'd kick in his proverbial mental doors and get him to talk to me.

The maybe-good-maybe-bad stuff was all about me and what I had learned about my power. I was Hecate. Not exactly. Like, I wasn't *her* her. I was her power reborn. Somehow. I'd unlocked her special, handy-dandy magics with my silver-key episode. I even had the key still, though I didn't know what it did besides rip into the heart of me, undo me, and reform me with powerful magics. Umar at-Tawil, the grim-reaper-looking guard who loved being cryptic, shoving it into my chest was an experience I definitely did not want to repeat. Ny knew little of the key and the cave and the back door to the Outer Gods' realm. He said it was his brother Yog's territory. After my weird encounter with his sire, Azathoth, on Kadath, I wasn't really keen to get into Yog's business. I kept it safely tied around my neck with a leather cord. I really hoped it wasn't needed again, but I wasn't about to push my luck and chuck it somewhere.

Overall, a few answers were given during the whole ordeal, but they led to a whole lot more questions, which would be the title of the book about my life anyway, so I was more than a little flippant about it all. Another day, another set of questions about who I was and what it meant. Whatever.

I had other worries. Namely, the bad stuff: Deb's funeral and Zeus lurking somewhere in the human realm. I was glad I had come back in time to go to Deb's funeral and give my condolences to her friends and family, but it was hard. No amount of condolences could erase the guilt and sadness I felt at her murder. She'd died because she was standing next to me, because I'd failed to take care of Wilbur months before… failed to even look into what he was planning. She'd died, Mia had been kidnapped and tortured, Nate had been traumatized, Gareth had been also, and all the people crying at the funeral had been a little more broken inside because I hadn't followed through with something. I may not have done the deed, but I also hadn't stopped it, which was all on me.

Zeus was the final bad note. He was out and about in my world. Probably close by, since we all knew he still wanted to get more from the Necronomicon—a.k.a. my sister Mia—and he wasn't too happy Ny and I were still around. He was planning something. What, I didn't know, but I wouldn't make the same mistake with this Other God that I had with Wilbur. I was on the offensive this time. I was set to kill a god, come hell or high water.

Post funeral, several of us went back to Warm Regards. It was a mess. Merry had cleared some of the debris from Wilbur's explosion, but she couldn't do a whole lot because insurance and cops and whoever else needed to investigate. Then we could clean up more and get contractors in to start fixing the big-ass hole in my kitchen. I'd need some new equipment too. Oh, and I had to fix the outer brick wall, which hadn't been damaged by Wilbur but disassembled with magic to make the gas-explosion theory more plausible.

Because of the same gas-explosion theory, and Merry's great advice on what I'd thought would be too much insurance years ago, it would all be taken care of by my insurance company. Merry and I had spoken with the adjusters after I'd returned. Things like employee loss of income, my loss of income, structural and business damage, state regulations, and a host of other things were discussed. I was present. I talked. It was important, I knew it was, but I was too mired in guilt about it all and too busy reeling from my time in the Dreamlands to think too much on it. Thankfully, Merry was there, like always, being the most helpful of sisters. She deserved a big ol' cake when I could cook in my kitchen again. Lots of cash too, for all the effort and time, but she wouldn't take that willingly, so cake it was.

While official people did official-type things, Warm Regards stayed in limbo. My employees would be paid for a time, which was my main concern. I was booted from my apartment until the city checked all the gas lines again and the inspectors and construction crew were finished. I'd been staying with Mia since she got back anyway because I needed to be as close as possible for my own peace of mind. After a few days, it was getting crowded, what with Mia and I playing teen sleepover in her bed, and Rich refusing to be anywhere but on Mia's couch. Her place wasn't big, and two grown women and a big-ass ghoul dude made it feel even smaller. I needed to figure out a different place to crash soon, but one problem at a time.

After arriving at Warm Regards, I couldn't bring myself to go into the kitchen and instead trudged down the alley and around to the cafe. Gareth had ridden with me from the funeral, and Harley and Merry had followed in Harley's sleek luxury sedan, which she whipped into the single open space in my back lot. Ny was already inside, holding the door open for me because he'd done his shadow-walking thing to get there first. No lock could hold him when he could command every shadow in this world and others.

I didn't even talk about how it was rude. I was too out of it to care. I flopped down at a table in the middle of the cafe, slumping in my conservative black dress and putting my head in my palms. I felt

Gareth take a seat beside me and scooch close. Ny's hands skimmed my shoulders, offering me silent strength and support without being too pushy or touchy. Merry and Harley pulled up to the table too. Merry, unlike everyone else, did push. She'd apparently learned from the Mia stuff too.

"Randy? Honey? Want to talk about it?"

Merry held herself tight, her dark hair pulled back so her big brown eyes and sweetheart face were on full display. She wore a flowy dress, like usual, except this one wasn't light and breezy. It was full and dark, a somber black that fit her mood even if it didn't fit her normal vibe. A lot of shit had her vibe off, and I was likely one of those things, given the way she looked at me.

I couldn't stand the thought of hashing it out with her right then, so I went with the truth. "No," I said, my voice sounding harsh and hoarse to my own ears.

"Sweetling," Ny said, sadness and pain lacing his words.

I heaved a sigh and went from slumped over the table to slumped with my back against the chair. "What exactly can I even say? Deb's gone."

Merry answered, "Yes. She was amazing, and I cared about her. You did too. But, honey, I'm afraid…"

She didn't finish as I looked at her, unblinking. Harley stepped in to be her ever-blunt self. "She and I are afraid you blame yourself for Deb's death. Which, if you do, is bullshit."

I cut angry eyes toward Harley, who sported her usual slacks and button-up combo, though they were in darker, more muted colors than normal. Looking at all the people circling, including a nervously jumping DD hovering around my head, I knew they were all concerned. Wrong, but concerned. "Not your call."

"What do you mean not our call? We can't see what happened as intelligent women and make an evaluation of the events?"

I threw a hand toward my sister. "She's never going to blame me for something like this. And you. Maybe you could blame me at one point, but not now. We're friends. Nearly family."

"As a friend, nearly a family member, I'd say it's my responsibility to call you out on your bullshit when I see it," Harley snapped back.

"Randy," Gareth said, taking one of my clammy hands in his. "What they're trying to say is you didn't kill Deb. Wilbur killed her."

"I'm not stupid, Gareth," I said, a little too harshly. I immediately regretted it, the instinct to bite back when I was on the defensive. Sometimes I couldn't help it. Regardless, they were all wrong in this one important way.

"I know I did not literally kill Deb. I also know I didn't stop Wilbur, in the moment or before he attacked. I let everything slide, and Deb died because of it."

"I was there, Randy. That's not what I saw."

My head whipped toward the door at those words. I hadn't even noticed Nate standing there. He must've also followed after the funeral.

"Nate. Damn. I'm sorry to say it, but you don't know what you saw or what it meant."

"I know a little more about magic now, thanks to Harley and Merry," he said as he straightened from his lean against the door and walked toward all of us. "I also know I saw you fight like hell for Deb, because of Deb. For me and Mia. None of this can be your fault."

"Randy, love," Ny said, snagging my attention. "You may not be able to see through your guilt currently, but what you say isn't logical, merely driven by pain. Understandable but faulty. By your reasoning, Gareth would be to blame for not stopping Wilbur when he was a young man. I'd be to blame for not realizing Zeus's machinations decades ago. There is blame that could easily be spread far and wide. The only concrete, correct assignment of blame sits squarely on the action. Wilbur killed Deb, not you."

I'd held it together at the funeral, thinking I didn't have the right to fully grieve my friend because of the role I played in her murder. She was lovely, light, smart as hell. A wonderful woman I would miss every day. When I thought of that, thought of what Wilbur had done and what I didn't, I couldn't hold back. In this space with these people, I didn't need to. I cried. Big, fat tears and throat-ripping sobs. I couldn't agree with them, not then. Maybe not ever, but my chest felt lighter with their words and DD's steady care down our connection. I didn't argue anymore. One problem at a time. My new motto. I needed to get through the next tragedy, or more like stop the next tragedy, then I could go to therapy or something. I doubted any therapist would believe this mess.

"Are there mage therapists?" I asked Harley when I could speak past the tears.

She smiled weakly at me. "We'll find out, Randy."

Good. I'd likely need one. Mia too. Hell, everyone in this room, probably. A magical therapist or counselor would make bank on our odd little circle. I chuckled at the idea, though my tears still trickled. A little dark humor in all the darkness never hurt.

# Two

WHEN MY TEARS SLOWED down and I was chattier with everyone, Merry gave Nate an encouraging nod. He moved closer to me and quietly asked, "Can we talk?"

"Sure, Nate," I said, blowing out a hefty chunk of air and shaking my head to help clear my tear-soaked mind. I felt Ny's hand squeeze my shoulder, so I craned my neck back to look at his face. Gods, even then, his beauty was almost too much to take in. The dark slash of his brows against his desert-kissed skin matched the dark worry in his deep-space eyes, and even in broad daylight, they swirled and pulsed with the light of unknown galaxies. He was darkness made flesh, from those eyes to the all-black suit he wore so well, and I'd always found comfort in the dark. Part of my magical quirks or whatever. I noticed his full mouth purse slightly. "Do you need time alone, or would you like us to be here?"

Always considerate, even if he was sometimes commanding. Guess it came with godhead. Maybe it was something I'd need to learn more about, but not at the moment. "I'm fine." Looking at everyone besides Nate in turn, I repeated myself. "I'm fine. Really. Maybe you all should go get some rest?"

Harley and Merry stood to leave, with Harley laying a firm hand in comfort on Nate's shoulder. Both women gave me a hug. Harley's was curt but effective, much like the woman herself. Merry's was hard and long, lingering so much, I became concerned. "How are you holding up, Merry Berry?"

"Not well, but I'm holding," she said, softly and full of hard honesty. "I'll be fine. I have Harley to see me through."

I looked at the mage, her hands shoved in her trouser pockets, her deep-brown eyes never missing a beat, her short, tightly coiled black hair and dark brows highlighting the glass-sharp slash of her cheekbones, the flare of her nose, and the fullness of her lips. Her face was model level, all hard angles and swooping curves, as was her flawless, lush, dark-brown skin. She was as fiercely beautiful as she was smart and powerful, and she was the one person who might possibly deserve all the soft love and care of my sweet Merry, mainly because she would return it in her own way. She caught and held my look, like she understood the direction of my thoughts. When Merry stepped away from me to look at Harley with a weak smile, the mage reached out a strong arm to engulf my sister, bringing her to stand at her side.

"Need us for anything, you know where we'll be," she said, before steering Merry out the door.

Gareth, his hazel eyes slightly darker than normal but still trained on me as always, stood from the table. His long blond hair was pulled back in a tight bun at the nape of his neck, slicked down so it looked darker than its usual sunny yellow. I matched his stance and reached to give him a deep hug, wrinkling his suit—a new look for him. It was a deep navy color, and for a second I wondered if he wore it to match my eyes. I didn't think too long on it before his big, muscular arms hugged me back, seeping a little of his calm comfort into me, which I more than appreciated.

"I'll see you later?" I asked after long beats soaking in his warmth.

We'd briefly discussed my sleeping arrangements because I'd decided to give Mia and Rich some space. Ny had assured us his place was plenty big for me, him, and Gareth if we wished to stay with him, all together. As I was more than curious about where Ny existed outside of my sight, and worried about how Gareth was handling his time in the Dreamlands, I'd jumped at the first invitation into his space. Gareth had also agreed, though he seemed ambivalent about it. "Yes, Randy. I'll meet you at Ny's later tonight."

I gave a quick squeeze and a soft kiss on his full lips. I had to stretch to reach him even as he bent to meet me. His blond beard was slightly scratchy, more scraggly than normal, and I rubbed my hands against it as I pulled back. "Later, then," I whispered.

He turned to leave, and the worry now living in my stomach marked "Gareth's Ordeal" churned harder at the down slope of his usually straight and strong shoulders.

Ny was still at my back, and he leaned down to whisper, "We will help our Gareth too, sweetling."

"Sure will," I said, maybe a shade too forceful. I was tired of having the people I loved have traumatic shit happen to them.

"I texted you and Gareth my address," Ny said before planting a soft, chaste kiss to my temple. "Come to me when you are ready."

"Always do," I replied, and he gave a low chuckle.

"So you do, sweetling."

He didn't look back as he moved toward a dark corner of the café and stepped into a midday shadow, fading from view as I watched.

"That's just too weird," Nate said, causing me to jolt. All the good-byes and worries and innuendos almost made me forget why everyone had left and I'd stayed behind.

"Takes some getting used to," I muttered before sitting back down at the table. "Please, Nate. Ask whatever you need to ask. I'm good to answer, as long as I know the answers." He looked so young sometimes, and this was one of those times. His boyish face was more cute than handsome, his brown hair a little too floppy and wispy. His honey-brown eyes... Those eyes showed not age but a shitload of not-great experience. It made me remember what he'd already been through in his short years here. Now he had the idea of magic and what it'd mean for him and his future to deal with on top of everything else.

Nate looked around at the café, his throat bobbing as if his nerves made it hard to form words. "Harley and Merry told me the basics, like magic exists... some people have an affinity for it. Those with affinities who learn more about magic are called mages, and Harley and Gareth are mages, but you and Ny are something else."

"About sums it up. The Cliff Notes version, but I suspect you want more details?"

"A few, at least." He paused and said, "Did you know?"

I cocked my head in question. "Know what?"

"I was magic or whatever."

"I knew something. My shadows responded to you. I don't know a whole lot about magic myself. I've known some things about it all my life, but it's only been in the past year I've started to learn about my powers and really hone them."

"Is it why you hired me?" He looked even more nervous to ask that question, and I reached out to take his hand.

"I hired you because you had good recs, you seemed like you'd fit in well here, and you made me a truly inspired dessert when I let you loose in my kitchen. I was new to the magic business myself, so it was something I noticed but it didn't really factor."

He nodded, bowing his head so he didn't meet my eyes. "I'm sorry I didn't know more..." His voice cracked before he could finish his sentence, but the direction of his thoughts was clear. Seemed Nate was left with a big scoop of survivor's guilt too. Even if I couldn't handle my own at the moment, I was more than ready to take down someone else's.

I shot to my feet and moved around the table to sling my arm over his slim shoulders and squeeze. "You didn't, and it's not on you. There wasn't any way you could harness magic unless one of us magic folks talked to you about it sooner. I maybe should have said something, but I was busy with my own intro to all this and didn't even know if it was my place."

"Harley also said a lot of people find out because of traumatic events."

"Yep. It's how Gareth learned about his affinity, though it isn't the case for Harley. I kind of knew I was magic all my life, but I didn't really get into it until recently, when I was nearly kidnapped by an evil cult."

"For real?" he asked, shaking his head. "What the hell's been going on in your life?"

I gave a harsh, mirthless laugh. "Right? Shit's been crazy for the past several months, believe me. I'm almost as new to it all as you."

His chest rose, held, and fell before he asked his big question. "Could you, you know, teach me some stuff?"

I squeezed him again, hating to say what I had to say. "No, honey. I can't. I don't know all that much myself. Also, I'm not a mage. I'm something else entirely."

"What?"

"Well, I don't rightly know. I'm a goddess reborn, whatever that means. I'm still learning too."

"Can I learn with you?"

I stared at him a moment, really considering his question. He deserved to learn, to explore his own power and affinity with magic. However, being around me and my swirling shitstorm maybe wasn't the best thing for him as he learned. I didn't want to reject him. He'd had plenty of that from his bigoted family before he even learned about magic. I wasn't going to add to it.

"I'm going to be totally honest with you. I don't think it's a good idea."

Nate stiffened under my arm, and I let him go but stayed close.

"Nate, look at me. This is not about you. If I knew more and was in less magic mayhem overall, I'd be more than happy to teach you whatever I knew. Right now, though, things are real dangerous around me. I can't in good conscience let you stick around and possibly get mixed up in it." My throat constricted. "Possibly die like Deb because you're near me," I said, the words coming out strangled.

He searched my eyes and nodded, apparently finding something there he believed, even if he didn't necessarily like the words. "Okay. I get it. I do. What am I supposed to do to learn more while you're off fighting whatever's out there?"

I stood, because I wasn't as young as Nate and my knees were starting to creak a little at all the crouching down. "Well, from what I gathered from Gareth's and Harley's stories, research was their first step, so you need books. I'm sure they'll point you in the right direction if you need it."

"Yes, please," he said, moving to stand himself. He looked me up and down, then quickly took me in a hug. "Thanks for being honest and helpful, even if it wasn't exactly what I wanted."

"I'll never be anything but honest with you, Nate."

"Good." He pulled back and moved toward the door. "I'll text Harley. Maybe Gareth too."

"Do. I know for a fact Harley has a few beginner mage books, because she had to get them for me not too long ago."

He opened the door and threw a look over his shoulder at me. He was so young still but had been through so much already—bigotry because of who he was attracted to, homelessness because of his shitty parents, and learning he was also magic somehow. It was a lot for a young man to take in, but he'd been forced to prove himself multiple times in life. My heart hurt he had to do it over and over again, but my brain knew he'd get through it. He searched my face, biting his lip for a second before he blurted, "Be careful, Randy. There's a lot of bad people out there in the normal world. Throw magic in the mix and..." He trailed off, not needing to finish. We'd both been there, together, when magic had gone tragically wrong.

"Got it, Nate. I'll chat with you soon. Promise. We'll have Warm Regards up and running when other things get handled. Until then, call if you need anything." I left unspoken the direction to call but not drop in. He knew the danger was real and closing in, and he was smart. He'd let us handle it before he came back. He'd also do his research and get himself prepared, because he now knew the things that slithered from the dark, and he'd learn to fear them as truly as he'd learned to fear the evil things people can do to other people. A hard lesson, but one not easily forgotten.

# Three

I drove over to Mia's place, a quick trip from Warm Regards. She hadn't come to the funeral. Not because she didn't mourn Deb, but because she was still skittish around people. She did okay in small clusters, but she'd nervously admitted she didn't think she could be okay with a crowd of mourners.

Totally understandable. She'd recently been through a hell of a lot of weird shit. I didn't even know the extent of it. I wasn't about to push her to attend Deb's funeral. I knew in my heart Deb wouldn't care. Mia could say her good-byes when she was ready, alone and at the cemetery. No need to force herself through a different type of traumatic experience.

Normally, I'd breeze into her home like she did mine. I had a key, so I could get in without much muss or fuss. However, Mia was still jumpy, and it now felt a little weird, given the way Rich and Mia were circling each other. I didn't think she was in a place for anything wild to happen yet, but getting an eyeful of my littlest sister naked with a ghoul wasn't exactly high on the list of images I wanted to have, so I waited patiently outside her door until it creaked open. I caught a glimpse of Mia scurrying back to her couch as I slowly entered.

Mia's place was fully Mia. Nerdy movie and TV posters lined the walls. Gadgets and tech littered most surfaces. She had cases and cases of bookshelves too, all filled to bursting. Mia liked to read and she liked collecting books. It was not the same hobby, as she often explained in great detail if anyone asked her about it. I liked to read too, but not nearly as much. I read cookbooks for work stuff and loved a good romance in any flavor, but I read maybe ten books a year. Mia read at least one hundred, and she would talk your ear off about any one of them.

I was happy to see her e-reader face down on her glass coffee table. I hadn't seen her read in a long while, probably since all the Necronomicon business started for her. Another sign I'd ignored, I guessed.

I stood in the living room, facing Mia and Rich. Mia sat on one corner of her big, overstuffed brown leather couch, arms wrapped tight around herself. Her petite frame was burrowed into the corner like it could shield her, her legs tucked up and under her, her arms up and crossed at her chest, and her head hanging low with her slightly long pixie cut poking out in an untamed halo. It was a sight that made my heart stutter.

Apparently it had Rich feeling something similar, because he sat stiff and strained on the opposite end of the couch giving my sister puppy-dog eyes, which he did well because of who he was. Rich was Richard Pickman, a part ghoul from the Dreamlands who'd stepped in to help Mia when he'd caught a whiff of Ny's scent on her.

I'd had my own weird encounter with a bunch of ghouls while in the Dreamlands. I'd been kidnapped by a night gaunt and taken to them for what were probably nefarious reasons. They'd been scared of me though. At first I thought it was because I smelled like Ny, but they'd claimed it was something to do with the moon. They'd sensed my Hecate connection before anyone else. They were very werewolf-like, so it made sense. They'd been all big teeth and long muzzles, crouched and lanky frames, scroungy fur, and yellow eyes with the animal predator flash in the darkness. Not exactly cute and cuddly. More like huge, vicious, snarling Dobermans meets the Wolf-men.

Rich didn't look like that. I imagine he could if he needed to, but Ny'd told me he was part human. He had the leanly muscled body of a swimmer, a frame stretched tall and powerful from wide-ish shoulders tapering to narrow hips and built legs. All of it somehow still radiated strength and power. His face was also narrow and slightly pinched, his features tight and stretched across a face I imagined could look haughty or vicious in equal measure. There was something a touch elvish about the sharpness of his features, although his ears weren't pointy. His wispy light-brown hair was long and pulled back in a man bun at the nape of his neck. His eyes were moon gray and had the same predatory flash as those of Ny and the other ghouls, sometimes turning green or red when light skittered across them in the dark. They were also keen, assessing. Rich wasn't overly talkative, but he watched, and I could tell he took in every detail with intent and interest.

Right then, all his ghoulish intent and power was focused on Mia, who had somehow made herself smaller on the couch.

"Mia? How are you doing?" I asked gently, plopping my purse and keys on the coffee table. I stayed standing so I could see them both at the same time. I asked Mia, but I wanted to see what Rich thought too.

"Not great, sis," she mumbled before closing her eyes tight and letting out a huge sigh. Quickly, as if forcing herself to get the request out, she said, "Can you call Gareth and Ny? Get them to come over. I... I need to talk about the Dreamlands."

I nodded, not knowing what to say. I wanted her to talk about it. We all needed her to talk about it, if we wanted to get the jump on Zeus and his desire for the Necronomicon. Despite the need, I didn't want this: the raspy pain of her voice, the jerky, small movements of her body, and her attempting to make herself smaller, like she wanted to disappear from view.

I gave her space because Mia sometimes needed to not be touched when she was feeling a lot, but I ached to hold her tight, rub her dark hair, and tell her she didn't have to do this now. What I wanted didn't matter. If she needed to be by herself with her body, if she needed to tell her story, I'd give her what she needed. Every day, whenever and wherever.

"Okay, Mia. You want them to come over now, or do you want to set a specific time for them to be here later?"

"Now, please. If they can."

They could. Or would. I'd make sure of it.

I dug my phone out of my purse and shot a text off to my guys to get there pronto.

"Done," I said, still clutching my phone in my hand. Before I could assure her they'd be there soon, two rapid-fire swooshes sounded. Ny and Gareth were on their way.

I GRABBED THREE DINING table chairs and put them at an arch around the coffee table so the guys and I could give Mia space while also focusing our attention on her. I tamped down my need to comfort and let Mia take the lead. She did a few minutes of breathing exercises to center herself before they showed, and it seemed to help. She unfurled and straightened, twisting her neck a few times, and then finally met my navy eyes with her dark-brown ones. She was putting on her mental armor to do what she felt like she had to do.

When Ny and Gareth showed up, at the same time of course, I let them in and told them to sit. For a second, Mia looked panicked, almost trapped, and she whipped her head around to look at Rich for help. He gave her a small, encouraging smile. A whole-ass conversation happened without words, and I couldn't tell if it was magic or simply connection allowing it to happen. Rich cut it off with a sharp nod, then turned to look at us.

"I'm going to start. Give my basic rundown and what I witnessed. That okay with everyone?"

No one objected, so he began by looking between me in the middle of our little arch of chairs and Gareth on the far end. "Ny knows more of my history, as we have been friends for decades, nearly a century. I won't give details now, as there is no need, but I am half human, half ghoul and chose to stay in the Dreamlands rather than live in the human world around the time I turned twenty-seven. It's been a very long time since I've returned, and even longer since I spent any period of time in my human form, so some of my descriptions and my words may be off. For that, I apologize."

I waved my hand and said, "No problem, Rich," which Gareth seconded before the ghoul began his story.

He spoke with a quick efficiency, laying out the basic plot points of how he got involved in it all. "I was going about my usual business when I caught Nyarlathotep's scent, which was somehow odd and mixed with things I did not recognize. I followed it, eventually finding Wilbur with a captured human woman in tow. I followed her because she was the source of the scent, and I assumed she had some important connection to the Prince because of it. When they reached a boat, I intentionally got caught so I'd be transported with them wherever they were going. By this time, I wished to protect Mia as much as possible.

Sadly, while in Kadath, there was little I could do but comfort her in our captivity."

Mia reached for his hand and gave it a firm squeeze when she whispered, "Your comfort was more than enough, Rich."

He shook his head, disagreeing or else disturbed by memories, but said no more. After a minute of silence, Mia looked down at the floor and spoke in rapid-fire sentences, getting her story out as quickly as possible. "I was unconscious for most of the trip with Wilbur, only awake here and there. I was tied up, gagged by some magic. When we reached the ship, I was released from the hold. Guess he figured it was safe. Rich appeared, and heard enough to make him a liability, so Wilbur took him too. Why he didn't just kill him, I don't know. I was constantly terrified of it, that they'd kill Rich to make me do something. I'd already watched one person die; I didn't think I could handle another one."

She paused, squeezing her eyes tight before she continued with her story. "I didn't see much of Kadath. Mostly just the dungeon place. Zeus was there as soon as we arrived, and he… went to work on the book right away. He tortured me with magic and physical pain in an effort to get the book from me. He tried to rip it out of me, but we both held strong, because fuck that guy. The book actively helped defend me—and itself, I guess. It dug in somehow, giving only trickles of spells and power away to hold him off. I think it only gave up enough to keep me protected, but I can't be certain what its intentions are or were. Now I feel more connected to it, like what we went through together made our bond even stronger or something."

She looked up, scanning our faces, and her body eased at whatever she saw there. "It was horrible, but we did okay. Made it until you three got there. Now, though, the book feels restless. I think it's because the part of itself it gave away to help save me is still missing. It liked being whole inside me, so now it's pretty damn unhappy it's no longer all up in my head."

It was a metric ton of oddness and trauma to take in, and all of it made my heart hurt for my sister.

"Mia, I'm so fucking sorry." Tears spilled down my face freely for the second time that day. I couldn't say anything else. How could I? She'd been through so much, felt and learned so much I couldn't understand and maybe never would, and all of it was on me.

"Don't," she whispered. "Please don't. I can't take you blaming yourself for all this. I'm an adult, I made adult choices, those choices had consequences. Sure, they were big-ass consequences we're all still dealing with, but you didn't do this to me. I did shit, it blew back on me, and now I have to deal."

I couldn't argue with her even if I wanted to argue. She needed support, not a bunch of bickering, so I shot Gareth a pleading look, and we each nodded, silently telling her we wouldn't press the issue.

"Mia, darling, you are beyond brave to continue such a journey. However, I must add, it is entirely outside the scope of what anyone has ever done. You are in uncharted territory." Ny was grave, serious... his regal posture and demeanor in full effect.

"Yep. I know. Little I can do about it now, but I know. I need to explore what it all means, and what my place is in terms of magic and the occult, on my own."

"Not entirely on your own," Rich said, a growl creeping into his voice.

Mia blinked at him, and her face softened a touch. "Correction. Not entirely on my own. I know keeping things secret led to a lot of not-great stuff, so I'm working on being more open and honest about my issues with everyone in our circle. Rich has agreed to stay here for a time and help me."

"We can help too," I said.

"I know, and you will, but you have your own magical mess to dive into, so you need to focus on that. Your Hecate powers are new and strong and are our best bet to get clear of all this. You three need to work on that. Rich and I can handle this. We'll eventually come together, I'm sure, because Zeus is here now and needs to be taken down for lots of reasons. All of us will have to be in on the fight." She paused, then stared at me. "I promise, Randy, we'll keep everyone in the loop. It's the only way we can do this from here on out."

"Too true," I said, thinking we all needed to be more open, more honest about what we experienced and felt. "I'll do the same. Are you going to have a similar talk with Harley and Merry, or do you want me to relay info?"

"I'll talk with them. Tomorrow. Now, I need rest."

I rose to give Mia the breather she needed. I silently gathered the few things I had stashed there and tossed them in my weekender bag. When I was ready, I couldn't hold back. I needed to hug my sister. I went around the coffee table with open arms, asking without really asking. Mia met me, colliding with my chest hard enough I felt it rattle my bones. We each squeezed tight for a long minute. I kissed the top of her head and whispered, "Love you."

"Love you too," she said, the sound muffled because her face was still smooshed against my body.

Finally, we let go, though not completely—never completely—and the guys and I made our exit, off to see Ny's place.

# Four

Ny usually shadow walked around, but because I'd never been to his place, he jumped in the car with me. Gareth followed behind on his bike with a stuffed duffle strapped down tight on his seat.

Ny gave directions, guiding me deep into German Village, the same place where we had our first encounter with Wilbur.

"You've been staying here in German Village the whole time?" I asked, slowing to navigate my car down the narrow, bumpy streets. The Mini Cooper was mini, but it still took effort to steer it through the tight maze of car-lined cobblestone roads.

"Yes," he said as he gazed out the window. "I felt attracted to this area after I was freed from the black church and found a dwelling rather quickly."

I didn't ask more right then, as he was turning me down sharp, short streets until we came to a tiny block of houses nestled in a central part of the neighborhood. Surprisingly, there was lots of open parking along his street, which was a rarity in this cramped area. There were a total of ten houses along the hidden lane, each quirky and unique. They were old but well maintained, with front yards shielded from the street, and all looked to also have backyards or patios. This equaled money, and lots of it, in an in-demand area like German Village.

Before I could fully get out of my car, Ny was around it with my bag loosely dangling from his hand. Gareth's bike had pulled in right behind us. He pivoted on one foot, bringing the other swiftly over his motorcycle to get both feet on the ground before he slightly shook himself. It made me chuckle.

"Rough ride?" I asked, thinking the brick streets had to be jarring on top of a motorcycle.

He muttered, "I've had rougher," and I let it be. He'd had an awful ride recently, and I didn't exactly want to remind him of it right then.

Instead, I looked at the beautiful little house Ny strolled toward. His sexy, loose-hipped walk looked slightly out of place in what looked like a house right out of a fairy tale. It wasn't called German Village for nothing.

A wrought iron fence encircled the yard, and a mismatched stone walkway led to the house. The small brick two-story had peaks and points in various places and an offset front door with an arched blue entryway. Bright mums bloomed in window boxes, and small bushes lined the property to give it more privacy. I noticed the walkway also curved around the side of the house, to what I assumed was a backyard or patio of some kind.

Ny didn't say anything as he entered without a key. It was Ny, who could open any lock with a shadow, so that meant little, but I did wonder if he bothered locking his doors. There wasn't anything scarier out there than him, so what would be the point?

DD was zipping back and forth, from the open door back to me, as I moved to follow Ny. Seemed about as excited to see the Outer God's digs as I was, but only barely. When I got close enough, it dashed ahead, disappearing inside the darkened doorway before I stepped over the threshold. The room I entered was open and sunny, with hella old-looking glazed windows dotting each outside wall. There was one enclosed space on the bottom floor, which I assumed was a bathroom. Everything else was a combined kitchen, dining room, living room, and study area. It flowed well and was richly furnished with a dark academia vibe that worked with the exposed brick walls and antique windows.

There wasn't a bedroom anywhere, but there was a staircase along one side, so the beds and such were likely up there. A set of black french doors stood along the opposite wall and led out to a small patio hedged in by an ivy-covered privacy fence with mostly empty flower beds at its base. A cool, swirling wrought iron table and chairs were set out in a prime sun-soaking spot.

I circled in place a few times, taking it all in as Ny said nothing. Finally, I whistled low and loud. "Nice," I said. "How'd you land this?"

Ny shrugged. "I convinced the management company I already had a lease."

"Don't you feel bad about that?"

"Feel bad for the rental management company or the hedge fund, which owns the house?" he asked, his dark brow arched and his smile a touch sharp.

Gareth laughed. "Fair enough."

"If there was a need, I could leave immediately, without any real consequence to any party involved."

I'd figured as much, so I had no desire to press the issue. Ny didn't take advantage of people who were in need, and really, I was fine with him sticking it to landlords and hedge funds, so I let it drop.

I walked toward the shiny, nearly new kitchen. It was built into the wall facing the street, with three smallish windows giving a good view of the yard and oddly deserted street beyond. A stainless-steel fridge was on one end. A matching dishwasher was on the other, right next to a deep, cream-colored porcelain farmhouse sink. Butcher-block coun-tertops in a rich walnut shade went well with dark-green upper and lower cabinets. The focal point for me though, smack in the middle of all of it, was a giant stove. Not just any giant stove. Ny had a freaking Aga.

"You're shitting me," I whispered before I ran over to the beautiful piece of cast-iron brilliance that was his Aga. Then I squealed, actually squealed, when I touched the smooth cream enamel, then ran my hands over the covering elements and felt a small bit of warmth seep through.

"It's beautiful," I whispered. Honestly, I never thought I'd see an Aga in person. It was like a dream come true. DD jumped around, from stove to me, almost bursting with happiness down our line, letting me know it was excited for me too.

I felt Ny's own unique warmth and sizzle behind me a split second before his hands moved to cage me between his magic heat and the fanciest stove I'd ever seen.

His hot breath puffed against my ear as he said, "I was informed this was the best oven available for home purchase and thought you might enjoy it."

"You bought it for me?"

I felt his head nod behind me, and I turned in his arms to look into his night-sky eyes. "You have Aga money?"

He laughed. "I've been on the human plane, off and on, for millennia. I have funds, for those times when it is not best to... let's say *convince* a person to give me something."

"Good to know, I guess, though this was totally unnecessary spending."

He nuzzled my jaw, a move filled with feline grace and affection, and softly spoke. "Your happiness is never unnecessary. I wish I could make you this happy for all eternity."

I melted a little and looked over at Gareth. There was no jealousy in his eyes, only his usual care, and I knew he wanted the same. The realization, and the love for them both pumping in my system, was the real kicker.

"You already make me happy. You both do. Extravagantly expensive appliances aren't needed."

"Agree to disagree," Ny purred, falling slightly into my body as he moved from nuzzling my cheek to kissing down my neck. My head fell back to give him room as he roamed with his lips, leaving a trail of scratchy fire with each nibble of lips and lick of tongue. DD swiftly disappeared, so I knew things were going to escalate.

The day had been a rollercoaster of emotions, most of them not good. The feel of his body, the lust and happiness and love it caused to swell in my own, made me desperate for more. I needed to feel something other than sadness and guilt and tears, much like the night in the Dreamlands. And Ny knew it too.

I opened my eyes halfway to search out Gareth. He stood several feet away, his hazel eyes dripping with lust. His jeans also looked a little tighter in certain areas. "Come here, big guy," I demanded, reaching an arm out toward him as Ny continued his trail of fire across my neck and chest. Ny stepped aside as Gareth came close, saying without words he wanted Gareth to take his place.

Gareth didn't hesitate. He moved in and followed Ny's licks and sucks with maddeningly gentle kisses. He stepped it up when he unzipped the back of my simple black sheath dress, letting the top half pool around my belly so he gained more access to my chest. He sprinkled slow, lush kisses along the tops of my breasts peeking out from my plain black bra.

I moaned, gripped his back tighter, and arched into his mouth, encouraging him to go further. When he unhooked my bra and tossed it to the brick floor, I locked eyes with Ny. The Prince stood beside Gareth, close enough to touch either of us, but he didn't. Instead, he slowly eased down the zipper on his dark jeans and reached into his boxer briefs to stroke his hard length. I gasped at the sight, but it quickly turned into a moan as Gareth took a nipple into his mouth and gave a hard suck.

"Ny," I called, wanting to touch him, or at least see him. With a sly, cocky smile, he only shook his head. "I watch," he purred as he stroked his dick more firmly in his hand.

Okay then. If that's how he wanted to play it, I'd let him go full voyeur. I focused back on Gareth and what he did to my body. He was lathing one nipple with quick flicks of his tongue before moving to give the other equal attention. It ratcheted up my lust, making my mind reel with need and desire.

After the day I'd had, I wasn't in the mood for long and slow. I needed immediate release, needed to feel something real and alive and powerful fueled by good emotions. I moved one hand from around Gareth and used it to awkwardly tug down my black cotton under-wear. I pushed them down as best I could, then kicked them off my feet as soon as I was able.

Moving Gareth up my body, I took his mouth in a searing, hard kiss. "I need you inside me." I panted before diving back toward his lips.

He didn't make me wait. He unzipped his jeans and pulled them and his boxers down past his hips, then hoisted me up on the kitchen counter. Under normal circumstances, I might have objected because of kitchen sanitation practices, but I was too far gone, too in need, to care. He gripped one of my fleshy, full hips as he lined his cock up with my entrance. I watched, fascinated by the look of him nearly inside me, but I glanced up when he didn't proceed. As soon as my navy eyes met his hazel ones, he thrust hard and deep, going full hilt in one forceful push.

I cried out but kept my eyes on his so he could read how good it felt for me. He muttered, "Fucking hell," as he stayed seated fully inside me and didn't move for a few beats.

I wasn't happy with slow and careful, so I started squirming on his dick, urging him to move. He did. After letting out a slow hiss of air at my squirming, he reared back, almost all the way out of my slick heat, and slammed home, causing another sharp cry to crawl up my throat. I gripped his shoulders tight, my trim nails digging into his flesh, and opened my thighs wider, letting him go as deep as possible.

He growled. Ny growled too, and I looked over at him finally, his intense stare focused on where Gareth and I were joined one moment, then trained on my face the next, all while he stroked himself. "Give him all of you, sweetling," he purred as I moaned with each sharp thrust of Gareth's hips.

It was hard and quick, exactly what I wanted at the moment. Gareth slammed into me without restraint, and I met his hips with mine, tilting back more to let him go as deep as possible, babbling incoherently about how good he felt inside me.

"Damnit, Randy. I'm almost there," he gritted out, taking his hand from my hip to hone in on my clit. It was the final push I needed, and I came screaming after his skilled fingers flicked over me for about twenty seconds. As I convulsed around his shaft, I bent forward and bit into his shoulder. I felt his muscles jerk and tense before he muttered, "Fuck," into my black hair.

My eyes were on Ny, who was rapidly stroking himself in his pants. I watched his face strain upward, his body bow and shudder, and I knew he came too. Only then did I focus on our magic swirling once again, the shadow and night and moss green combined into our own little sexual aurora borealis.

After he stuttered out a breath, he touched Gareth's arm to get his attention. Gareth, still seated inside, turned his head as it rested on top of mine, so I could only assume he looked over at Ny.

"May I?" Ny asked, before gesturing toward Gareth, who breathed deep before landing a sweet kiss to the top of my head and pulling himself off and out of me. I missed the feel of him immediately, though a slight ache lingered. Enough of an ache to remind me he'd been there and make me hope it'd stick around for a while.

Gareth stepped back slightly and finally croaked out, "Yeah, sure."

Ny didn't say more. He did his thing, gathering the magic and pushing it into Gareth, charging him like a battery. Usually there was leftover magic Ny had to put somewhere, like his magic pocket watch thingy, but Gareth took it all this time. Didn't know what that was about, but I was too blissed out to ask magic questions.

I hopped off the counter and pulled the top half of my dress back into place, so I wasn't totally naked in the kitchen, and shimmied off the counter. "Okay. Where's your cleaning wipes?"

Ny looked at me, blinking in confusion.

"You know? Cleaner? So I can wipe down the counter after our rather unsanitary activity."

Again, a look of utter confusion. "Use your shadows, sweetling" was his reply.

My mind skidded to a halt. "What?" I asked.

Ny shrugged his shoulders. "Use your shadows to clean the area."

"Okay. Later we'll have a conversation about you holding out on shadow-cleaning services. Right now, I'm unsure what antibacterial and antimicrobial shadow cleaning is. If you don't have cleaning wipes, we'll pick some up at the store. Do you have stuff to make breakfast for dinner?"

Ny again shook his head in confusion, and I sighed. That's what being an all-powerful Prince of the Dreamlands did to a being, made them forget the little things. "Looks like we're going to the store for multiple things. Let me clean up real quick. Gareth, could you have a look around the kitchen, maybe note the basics Ny does and doesn't have?"

Gareth nodded and pulled up his pants before rummaging through cabinets. I grabbed my weekender bag and moved toward the bathroom to clean myself up and change into some athleisure wear, the best option for both grocery runs and cooking in a beautiful new kitchen.

# FIVE

It was late, like three o'clock in the morning, a time I'd once heard someone call the witching hour. I'd dealt with one witch before and knew they didn't need a designated hour to cause a ruckus. We'd had tasty breakfast for dinner, including fluffy buttermilk biscuits made in Ny's gorgeous oven. There was chatting, but mostly we were all tired from a long and emotional day, so we trekked upstairs after Ny invited us to follow him.

The bulk of the second floor was a bedroom, with two smaller doors along the far wall. My guess was another bathroom and a closet. Ny needed to hang his leather jacket somewhere. Mostly it was bedroom, with a massive, bigger-than-California-king bed smack in the middle. I made a halfhearted joke about Ny's penchant for huge beds and got a few chuckles. With tired eyes and a full belly, I stripped down to my underwear and crawled to the middle of the bed, rightfully assuming the guys would follow me. Garth's calm hit my back, Ny's power sizzled down my front, and I snuggled deep, content between the two.

Content, that is, until I woke with a start sometime later and Gareth's side of the bed was empty and cool to the touch. I grumbled a little, rubbed the sleep from my eyes, then groped around the dark until I found Gareth's discarded tee. DD, who'd been absent since our non-cooking kitchen escapades, was floating calming at my side, so I wasn't too worried about the mystery of one missing dude. Slipping

Gareth's shirt over my head, I took a quick side trip to the bathroom, then slowly made my way downstairs in search of my big guy.

I found him in the study nook of the open space downstairs, surrounded by books but not looking at any of them. He was motionless, staring off into space.

I tiptoed up to him and whispered his name a few times, to no response. When I reached his side, I snapped my fingers in his face and said in a low but sharp tone, "Yo, big guy. You there?"

Gareth blinked rapidly and shook his head, his hazel gaze unfocused until he zeroed in on my face. "Randy" was his only reply before he brought his big hands up to rub down his face.

"Hey," I said, grabbing a small wooden chair from beside the desk and scooting it closer so I could grab his face in my hands. "You good?"

"Fine," he mumbled, and I dropped my arms to cross them at my chest.

"Obviously not, Gareth. Try again."

He released a long, loud breath. "Killing a person—even if the person isn't fully a person and they deserve death for what they have done and would do—isn't easy for me."

I paused in thought before answering softly but firmly, "It shouldn't be, Gareth. It should be hard, and it should be on your mind. Maybe you don't need to be exactly haunted by it, but it is something... something not so great." I wasn't being the most articulate, but my own guilt over Macy welled up in the moment, threatening to choke me. "I think it makes us human, and if not exactly good, then at least feeling, people."

He nodded and went on. "Wilbur was an albatross. The thing I focused on, the thing weighing me down for so many years. Hell, I still don't even know exactly why he targeted me and my friends on that camping trip so long ago. I didn't bother to ask. Now, he's gone. I'm happy he's gone, glad he can't hurt anyone else I care about anymore." He shook his head, as if rattling loose the thing he didn't want to say. "It's left me feeling unmoored. I don't know exactly what to do with myself."

"Wilbur was your focus for a long time, big guy. He's no longer a threat or an enemy to work against because of his own evil-ass shit biting him in his, well, evil ass, but he's a non-entity now. It makes sense you'd feel a little lost after getting past this big looming, horrible thing."

We sat in silence, him twisting his hands in his lap, before he said, "It might be more, and this part scares me the most. The void I went into, it wasn't what you saw. Not exactly. Hell, it wasn't even what I saw when I first saw it or was submerged in it. It was a breathing thing, endless, without time or space or feeling. I drifted there for what felt like forever and no time at all. I came out cold somehow."

This was way beyond my paygrade. Gareth was usually one of the people who helped me understand the magic mess I didn't know anything about. "Are you sure it's something magical and not just emotions messing with you?"

"Not one hundred percent, no. I know I can hold more power now. Beyond that, I can't be sure until I test myself more."

"I noticed the extra battery storage earlier," I said.

A ghost of a smile passed his lips. "My magic works fine, so far at least. Haven't had much chance to test out on any complex spells. Still, something feels off. Different. I feel somehow empty."

I slumped back in my chair. "Well, big guy, I think we all feel empty sometimes. Numb to things. There's been a lot happening in a very short amount of time. Could be you haven't processed everything and need a break to work through your shit, which would be totally understandable. Or, hell, maybe you even need to process in some magical way I don't know anything about because I'm clueless about the magic stuff most of the time." I leaned forward again, getting up in Gareth's downturned face. "I know this, though. I know you're a badass at magic and fighting. A fierce protector. A good man. Someone I love." I paused, smirked, and added, "I don't love just anyone, you know. You gotta have something special in there for that to happen."

I tapped his chest, and he clasped his hand over mine, bringing it up to kiss my palm, then cradle his own bearded cheek in my hand. "I love you too, Randy. At least that breaks through the numbness."

I didn't really want to say it, but I needed to. "The lovefest is great, believe me. But I gotta say it: this one thing can't be your purpose. I can't be your purpose, not your sole purpose at least. I can, and want to, be a part of what you do in the future. How you find your bearings again and start doing something else amazing with your time and energy and magic."

"You need a good deal of help right now, Randy."

"I know that. Gods, do I know that. I'm more than willing to take your help too. So is Mia. So is Ny, I think. And Harley may be gruff, but she's got a soft spot in her heart for you, you know. We all need you in our own ways, but you need you too. You need your own purpose, something for you. Something to give you direction, to take the numb and turn it into drive. Something your own, or at least not fully tied up in another person."

I heard "so wise, sweetling" whispered from the corner of the room where the staircase loomed, and I started at the sudden inclusion of the third person in our little group. Ny stepped into the dim shafts of light, blending in somehow, being of and not a part of as he always was, something bigger than and the exact same. A person of time and space and stardust who'd somehow landed in my life.

Gareth grunted, but it wasn't in anger or annoyance. It was a bro-ish greeting even though neither of these men were bro-ish.

"Eavesdrop much?" I asked, mostly because he'd scared me a bit.

"Sorry, love," he replied, bending down to give me a swift kiss on the forehead when he reached our little clutch. "I'll stomp like a human next time."

I snorted but quieted when Ny turned dark, night-sky eyes on Gareth, giving him a full once-over. "Friend, the void has changed your capacity, but not you. There may well be other additions from the time spent there, but nothing detrimental. We can explore together if you wish, but I think Randy may be right. You need to process, as you humans are now so fond of saying."

Gareth didn't say anything, so Ny continued, situating himself so he gave the other man all his intense attention. "Take some advice from a very old being, my friend. As you grow, purpose grows. Evolves. Ebbs and flows across your sliver of time and space. You will find purpose again, and knowing you, it will be righteous and grand."

Ny landed a large hand on Gareth's shoulder as the big guy slumped but nodded, clearly taking in what we were saying.

"Very well," Ny said with a definitive nod. "Now, let us return to bed. Night is good for confessions and conversations, but also good for other, far more pleasurable endeavors."

I shivered and took the hand Ny offered, rising as Gareth did, and the three of us went back to bed, back to each other's arms and warmth and magic, back to feeling a little something through the chaos of our intertwined lives.

Gareth left early in the morning for his regular human job at OSU's library. I gave him a hearty kiss good morning and good-bye. I, sadly, had nowhere to be because Warm Regards would remain closed until inspectors and contractors and whoever else poked around the place more. I could tell them not to bother. Magical attacks weren't happening there again, but they were all worried about gas leaks instead of evil-magic shit. Better to let the story ride, even if it meant waiting around without anything to do but obsess over said evil-magic mess.

I did have something I needed to dig into, and it wasn't just the tasty food I had squirreled away in Ny's lovely kitchen.

The Outer God himself was lounging in his particularly regal way, draped across a chair at his dining table, watching me as I banged around and gathered and reheated things. Once I sat down with a small plate and some butter and jam, I prepared my breakfast, then took a big bite of leftover biscuit before I said, "Tell me about Hecate."

Ny didn't blink at the demand. He likely knew it was coming, seeing as he was the only being I knew who knew Hecate when she was alive.

"Hecate was an Other God, an Earthly God. A Titan, in fact, which technically means she predated many of the Other Gods. Not all, mind you, but many. She did, however, outstrip all in terms of power—power she expressed while a goddess on Earth and the power she kept over the millennia, even after her move to the Dreamlands."

It was a decent start, but I needed more. I had a whole mental checklist of questions hanging out in my brain, so I went down the line. "What was she goddess of, exactly?"

"When a Titan, or even before Titans to be more accurate, she was ruler of sky, earth, and sea."

"So not much at all," I quipped as I took another big bite.

Ny quirked his lips at my sarcasm and moved right along in his explanations. "Once she stepped aside, for other Titans, then Zeus, she was goddess of night, magic, and darkness—plus all such things that entailed, like witchcraft, the moon, shades and spirits, even necromancy."

"The ghouls responded to the moon thing. I had it even when they met me?"

"You've likely had it dormant inside you all your life, sweetling. The ghouls were simply the first to truly recognize that particular side of your power."

I nodded, moving a bit to the more personal. "How did you know her?"

Ny studied my face a moment before he continued in his cool tone. "We were never lovers, Randy, if that is your true question. Not that she was not gorgeous. Hecate had a dark beauty and compelling presence much like you. There was, however, a particular coldness about her you lack, which I'm very thankful for. No, we were never lovers, but close allies for millennia. Friends even, to a point. However, I have my suspicions she was one of my sire's lovers."

I spit a bite of my buttery biscuit all over his pristine dark-wood table at the revelation. "Excuse me? You mean to tell me Azathoth, the Big Dude in Charge, was lovers with Hecate, the goddess who I now somehow have the powers of?" I didn't know what was more shocking: the idea of big scary King Azathoth with lovers or the fact my power might be intimately connected to Azathoth in a way I was not comfortable thinking about too much.

Ny's muscles were tense, his silent answer curt and stiff. It apparently didn't please him either. "I suspect this is why Azathoth showed his face at Kadath when you were in attendance."

I slumped. "Do you think..." I couldn't even finish the thought. There were too many possibilities, and not many of them were positives.

"I believe he wished to meet you. He knew, somehow, whose power you possessed even before we did. I do not think he was trying to seduce you." The last two words were gritted out though, which made their intention fall a bit flat. Ny might not think it, but he still worried about it, or at the very least did not like the idea at all. Which was weird, because the Prince definitely did not have a problem sharing. I think he liked it even. Maybe he just didn't want to share with his sire, and I didn't really blame him. Azathoth was too much of everything to make me ever feel comfortable around him. Weird, I know, given I slept with an Outer God on the regular, but Ny and I had a connection—emotional, physical, and magical—which made me see him as him, not as some all-powerful being I didn't know or trust or love.

"He definitely knew before you did?"

Ny's jaw dropped a bit and hurt flashed across his starry eyes at the accusation, but I had to ask. "I've never lied to you, Randy. I had inklings, wisps of suspicions, especially the longer we spent in the Dreamlands, but I never knew. It has never been witnessed in all of eternity, godhead power reborn in a human. Did not know it was possible."

I swallowed down a bit of orange juice and asked, "Am I human?"

"You've always been human, will always be human. Now we simply know where the extra magic comes from, even if we don't know how or why."

This was getting more toward the meat of worry, the worm wiggling in the back of my mind. "I'm not an Other God?"

Ny looked thoughtful for a moment. "I suspect you are both, somehow. Wholly new and unique in existence."

"Will I become godlike? Change?"

A finger stroked the back of my hand, a zap of power, familiar and tingling, grounding me. "You will stay you, always. Because of who you are and who you keep by your side."

His words were little comfort in a mass of confusion, but I'd take comfort however I came by it. Before I could ask more, my phone bleeped, notifying me of a text. I glanced down and saw it was from Nate, and curiosity got the better of me, as we'd seemed to agree to keep a little distance just yesterday.

Nate wanted Gareth's number. He'd talked briefly with Harley. She'd said she'd bring him books, but he should contact Gareth if he needed to talk with someone one-on-one. I didn't know if Harley was too busy, not wanting to teach, or also had a mind for Gareth's weirdness since returning, but the idea of Gareth becoming a mentor for Nate suddenly seemed perfect for both of them. We'd discussed purpose last night, and knowing Gareth's personality, teaching new mages might fit the bill. I shot the contact info over to Nate without hesitation.

"What has put such a smile on your face, sweetling?" Ny purred, angling his head to try to see my phone screen.

I turned it around to show him. I had nothing to hide from him—either of my guys, really. "Nate wants to talk to Gareth about mage-y things. I think it might be perfect for them both. Give Gareth a project to latch on to and help Nate out at the same time."

"Agreed," he said in his imperious tone, as if it'd been his idea or something.

I snorted and placed the phone on the table as I stood. "I'm done with my interrogation for now, but reserve the right to ask more questions later."

"Of course."

Leaning over, I gently touched Ny's cheek with a jam-slicked finger. "I'm all sticky with jam. Seems you might be too. I think we need a shower."

A rumble of a purr echoed in the room, and I chuckled. He definitely liked the idea.

# Six

Sadly, before I even hit the bathroom door, a phone rang in the space. I looked at mine on the table, but it was dark. Apparently, it was Ny's. Weird, because I'd thought I was the only person to ever text or call the dude.

He growled in a not-sexy way at the interruption, then reached in his pocket as I marveled that his phone actually fit in those deliciously tight jeans he liked to wear. His brow wrinkled when he saw who was calling and he stood swiftly, saying, "Rich."

He'd put it on speakerphone, and as soon as it clicked, I heard a terrible whimpering cry muffled behind the sound of Rich saying, "We need you, Ny. And Randy. Now."

I didn't hesitate. If Rich was calling and some weird shit was going on in the background, said weird shit definitely involved Mia, so I was there. I rushed to grab my car keys from the small table beside the door, but Ny's hand was on my shoulder in a flash, holding me back. I whipped around to stare daggers at him. Surely he knew we needed to motor.

He shook his head at me as he said into the phone, "We will be there directly," before hanging up and sliding it back into his pocket.

"In order to do that, Ny, we have to leave. Now."

"Yes, Randy, but why take the car when we have a far more efficient way to travel?" He gestured toward a shadowed corner. I wanted to smack myself upside the head. Of course. It was only us. We both could shadow walk, which would get us to Mia's way quicker. No pesky stop lights or traffic.

I hesitated long enough to say, "I've never traveled that far when shadow walking."

"You are more than capable, especially now. Start as you know, with intention and focus. I will guide us if you keep hold of my hand. I will not leave you behind. You may well find you flow through shadows like water with your newly unleashed power."

I nodded, tamped down questions about shadow walking and Hecate, and secured my hair up in a messy knot with the hair tie on my wrist. Whatever we were about to walk into would likely mean I needed my hair out of my face. "Let's do this."

Ny took my hand and led us into the corner, melting away bit by bit, until the only remaining solid fleshy bits were his fingers wrapped around my hand. Then his hand and my hand followed into fading. I was concentrating, doing all Ny had taught me before, and even putting extra intention behind it, coaxing my body to become shadow, which it did easily—almost happily, like it was made for this, the deep bass of magic in my gut thumping a joyful rhythm at the prospect of becoming one with darkness.

I cut through the shadows like a shark swimming through deep, dark seas, without pain or jarring or fear, from point to point, following Ny's lead. When I'd shadow walked before, the pain had been so distracting, I'd had little brain power left over to look at the shadows all around me. I'd dissolved and become back then, coming undone and redone. This, though. This process felt more fluid, more natural, like I was returning rather than forcing my way in. Shedding one skin to reveal another, not different me but a different form of me. The rightness of it allowed me to finally see the swirl of shadow around me with a kaleidoscope of varieties of black. Some were so dense, it looked like the void Gareth had tumbled into; some felt and looked like DD, who still clung close to my side even through all this. Some verged on gray, a black speckled with lightness so the darkness around it looked richer and more pronounced. In the middle of it all, too, was magic. Sparks of things I didn't know but could briefly taste on the tip of my tongue, almost like the memory of a good meal. We were going too quickly for me to stop and savor all the flavors, to even distinguish what was there, but I wanted to at another time.

The more I sensed and experienced, the more confident I became. I knew I could very easily do this on my own. I shook off Ny's hand and moved to his side. I saw the shadow of a smile in the darkness, Ny's lips curving at me stepping up instead of following behind, and we jumped from shadow to shadow so swiftly, it became a fluid motion to my eye rather than a series of leaps.

Then Mia's small porch was visible ahead, and we slowed enough to melt back into reality, once again without effort or pain on my part. I didn't have time to think of anything else before I heard a sharp yelp, followed by a worried bark of "Mia!"

I ran into Mia's place, and once we were inside, I froze at the scene in front of me. Rich was pacing the living room like an agitated animal, letting out a deep, rumbling growl as he focused solely on Mia in the middle of the floor.

My sister was writhing on the ground, her arms curled hard against her chest, her hands claw-like and straining as if fighting something. She twisted and turned, then bowed off the floor for a moment. A few yelps and almost distant-sounding screams echoed in the space, but it didn't match her look. Her face was distorted, her mouth stretched wide and her throat straining as if she were screaming at the top of her lungs.

"Do something," Rich said with a snarl.

Ny kneeled at her side and skimmed his hands over her form, trying to figure out what had Mia in its grip. I didn't need to be that close because I smelled it first, then tasted it on the air, a thing like burnt hairspray and brine and bad meat mixed up together. Then I saw it. There were thick, wispy gray tendrils shot through with blue sparks circling around my sister, but not exactly. It was almost like an overlay in my sight, something there but not. Something I could see as a hazy film over reality. I instinctually knew it wasn't just the effects I was seeing, but the actual spell. DD shaking and agitated at my side and the frequency of the thrum of magic in my gut both told me a spell had been cast on my sister, and what I was seeing was the damn thing trying to wriggle its way through to whatever end the spellcaster had in mind.

Another shrill telephone rang. This one was familiar. I closed my eyes, imagined the old wall phone from our childhood kitchen, and picked up the line. Merry must've felt my uncertainty and fear and worry all mixed together, but I didn't have time to talk. I said, "Mia's in trouble, but stay the hell where you are. Ny and I have this," before slamming my mental phone back on the mental kitchen wall.

I breathed deep, shook my head, and came back to reality. Then, I acted on pure instinct. I had DD wrap itself around Mia in a bubble and contract slowly so it snared all those stinky, foul-tasting tendrils in its shadowy grasp. Once it was good and caught, I yanked experimentally. Mia writhed more, but the spell trembled and wavered, so I knew I was on to something.

Ny whipped toward me and yelled, "Randy, don—" but it was too late. I needed the damn thing gone and off my sister, so I pulled hard, ripping it off her like a Band-Aid.

Mia's scream was piercing, but thankfully, it stopped almost immediately. Mia wasn't under attack any longer. She was orchid pale and trembling but looked physically okay.

Rich was on his knees, shouldering Ny out of the way so he could scoop my sister up in his arms. He stroked a small bit of her black pixie cut from her forehead and asked, "Are you okay?"

She managed to croak out, "Yes," her voice harsh and low.

Ny rose, unconcerned with Rich's brushing him aside. He only had eyes for me. Kind of angry-looking eyes, actually, but he didn't get to say anything before Mia started to talk.

"Zeus," she stuttered out. "It was Zeus, trying to get me. The Necronomicon. Whatever. Trying to get us, transport us to where he is. He couldn't fully get hold of me because the book defended me, or itself at least. Held him off."

Ny's lips moved as if he spoke, but I couldn't hear his words. My vision filled with black. Don't know if my eyes matched, but all I knew was anger, a dark, seething black anger like a cannonball sitting square in the middle of my chest, making it hard to breathe, to think, or to understand anything else but a driving need to do something. To do harm to Zeus for once again fucking with my sister. It was much like the time Starry Wisdom had threatened to take me and my sisters from the movie theater parking garage. It was black, hot rage uncurling in every part of my body, coloring my world, blinding me to everything else.

DD had the spell wrapped tight, and I studied it hovering waist-height off the ground, my head somehow parceling out what it was and what I could do with it. I could see the barely-there blue lines echoing outward, a ghost of a path away to somewhere else. If he had planned to take her, there had to be a predetermined destination mixed into the spell somehow.

Without thought, without concern for whatever it was Ny was now talking about at my side, I told DD to release it, wrapped the spell tight around my fist, and concentrated on the trail of breadcrumbs the spell left behind. I didn't move physically. No. I dream walked in pure daylight without being asleep, seeing myself form into my dream-walking image, with my robe and spear and everything, then shifted my mind so I watched at the edge of the room as the others yelled at my clearly-zoned-out physical body. I couldn't worry about that right then, because even in my dream form, I was seething with a dark, dangerous rage. I twisted and pulled, then closed my eyes, focusing all my intent on the spell giving me its final destination.

The blue sparks bucked, trying to shut me out, but I wanted in too badly. I wrapped them tightly in my fist and yanked with my mind, stretching it taut until it finally relented, opening a way through some unknown channel for me. I closed my eyes and leaped toward the end point, without thought or care.

When I opened them again, I was floating with a speck of DD at my side, hazy in a real-world place, smack in the middle of a sleek and modern apartment. In front of a bank of floor-to-ceiling windows, staring out at downtown Columbus and the Scioto River below, Zeus stood with his hands loosely clasped behind his back. When he turned to see me, surprise flashed on his face for a millisecond before a slightly mocking smile hit his lips.

"Ah, Miranda. Not the Carter sister I wished to see right this moment, but I cannot say I'm overly disappointed."

Shock was there, sure, but anger at the audacity of this dude overrode almost everything. It definitely overrode the shrill landline sound in the back of my mind. Merry would have to wait for an update from me. I needed to focus on the god in front of me and how, exactly, I'd beat his ass.

# Seven

Zeus was bathed in the light from the wide expanse of windows. In Kadath, he'd been dressed in robes and precious metals and jewels, looking like what I'd imagined a Greek god would. Or maybe it was what they always had looked like, and it was what we humans remembered somewhere in our lizard brains after thousands of years. I'd been decked out in finery too, but it'd had a modern human bend to it, to make me comfortable in the new place.

Here and now, we'd somehow reversed. I was once again in my dream-walking garb: the dark, flowing robes hugging the more-than-ample curves of my body, black sandals cradling my feet, and a darkly shining spear weighing heavy in my clenched fist. Kind of. Not really. All of me appeared slightly hazy and misty, not fully solid, like I was a dream myself.

I wasn't completely stupid when it came to magic stuff. I kind of appeared like Ny had when I'd first seen him, the one time at Heatwave, so I thought I could be doing some form of astral projection. DD was here, at least some of it, still connected to me. Whatever I'd done had allowed me to bring it along too, which wasn't always the case when I dream walked places. I was hazier and more shadowy, less solid, but I was still me, or at least the version of me in my Hecate look. Of all I'd seen and done so far, the astral projection bit seemed the most likely answer. Didn't really matter a whole lot in the moment, not for me. I had all eyes on Zeus, worried and angry over what the hell he was trying to pull.

Unlike me in my kind-of-there form, Zeus was all too real, and dressed to the nines, as my mom would say. He wore a full three-piece business suit, so immaculately cut it looked specifically made for his honed god body. The suit was storm-cloud gray, and the shirt and shiny pocket square peeking from his chest were sapphire colored and almost as shimmery as a gemstone. He looked serious and regal and in charge in the stark, rich apartment with its similarly sleek lines and cool tones.

His shock of light-gray hair was a little more tamed now, not flowy but cut to barely touch his collar and styled to fall back from his face. His beard was also trimmed close, showing more of the pale expanse of his white features, the wide set to his mouth, and the strong line of his jaw and chin. It was a twenty-first century style, and it looked good on his handsome face. It'd look better if the glint in his gray eyes wasn't so hard and his smile didn't crawl with mocking and dominance. Those two things made me want to punch him in his stupid mouth so I could muss up those modernized looks. Make him look more savage, like he actually was.

He took a step back and flung an arm to his left as he turned fully toward me. "Please, Miranda. Do have a seat."

"Randy," I hissed out between not-really-there clenched teeth. The rage I'd followed to this apartment cooled some with all the magic and newness and uncertainty. It simmered though, close to the surface, edged along by his smug looks and pompous attitude.

Zeus chuckled. "Of course. Randy. Again, please sit."

It was only then I really took in what was around us beyond the vague notion of modern, expensive apartment generalities. The place was sparsely and generically furnished. Everything existed in tones of white and gray, from ceiling to floor. There was a large open space with sections for sitting and eating. A dark hallway was off behind Zeus in the right back corner, past the wall of windows. To the left was a small kitchen, so new and gleaming, I knew it'd never been used. High end but ignored. Definitely not the heart of the place like a kitchen should be. In fact, the entire apartment felt heartless, soulless. Like its owner.

A quartet of sleek metal and leather chairs circled a low glass coffee table, which was where Zeus headed right then. I jumped when I finally looked behind me because I hadn't noticed the two men sitting there before Zeus walked toward them. They were men, not something more. Mages to be precise, a matching pair looking like the agents from *The Matrix*, except they glowed with the faint light of sigils peeking out from their stark black-and-white suits. One stared a little too hard in an oddly familiar way. Took me a minute before it hit me. I'd seen these men once a few years back, staring in a restaurant, then doing weird magic shit before I even knew what weird magic shit was. They were the dudes from Merry's birthday, the night of the tornado and all that had come with it.

Zeus again chuckled in his know-it-all way, apparently amused by my surprise or lack of understanding or both. "My associates. I do believe you have met in some capacity previously." Gods, I wanted to wipe his stupid flippant smirk off his stupid face.

"How?" I asked, my head swimming, trying to clear enough to get a broader view of this evil-magic mess I'd somehow been in long before I even knew I was smack in the middle of it.

Zeus unbuttoned his jacket and sat, smoothing his lapels as he did. "How do you think Starry Wisdom came to know of you, Randy? Came to this small city in the first place? It was luck, of course, that my human servants spotted you one evening, but all else afterward was planned, I assure you."

My anger sparked hot again, a dark flame consuming my questions, which caused shadows to roll in waves out of my hazy form, darkness snapping and crackling all around me. I refused to move. My form was locked down tight because I was ready to lash out, but also something in my head held me back, made me wait. I didn't know what I could do as a hazy figure. DD was also there, tied to me somehow, and I didn't want it hurt. I was impulsive, true, but I wasn't callous with DD or anyone I cared about, so I needed to tread lightly.

The Other God sighed and shook his head. "Randy. I truly do not wish to be your enemy. We are here and now because I wished it to be so. I want nothing more than to work with you, to help guide and mold you into your true potential. After all, Hecate and I were close, long before the time I ruled over all the gods on Earth."

"I heard she let you rule, which to me sounds like you didn't exactly rule over her as much as you pretend you could."

A flash of light streaked across Zeus's eyes. "You were not there to know or understand such things."

"Part of me was, apparently. A part of me that you seem interested in, and maybe even a little afraid of."

He let out a harsh crack of laughter. "Oh, dear Randy. I do not fear you. I could never fear you. Why would I fear a creature such as yourself? Someone born so very beneath me?"

"Obviously not born so far beneath you to escape your notice."

He raised a hand and twirled it in the air. "There is no reason to have such hostile debates, Randy. We are now both powerful beings who could help one another."

"I don't want or need your help, Zeus. In fact, I'd very much like you dead."

"Such harsh words for one so unsure."

"Not as unsure as you think."

He shrugged. "I have no need to worry. With the Book of Knowing—"

"Which you can't even use," I said, interrupting him. "Might as well go ahead and give that back to Ny while you're at it. Takes real power to use the thing."

Another flash of the eye and Zeus's mouth curved down in a scowl. "I will soon best the Prince and his book. Both books."

My rage welled again, black and hot, and I seethed, bringing back to the whole reason I was even there in the apartment with the arrogant prick. DD jumped, also agitated on behalf of me and Mia. "Stay the fuck away from my sister."

Zeus, a coy tease in his voice, said, "But she is so lovely, inside and out."

"Enough of this banter crap," I said. "We can fight now, or you can leave and abandon your shitty plans, whatever they are. I don't care. I came because you tried to take my sister. I'm done with your bullshit back-channel attacks."

"Randy, do you even realize what you have? Your magical abilities, the book, access to and the trust of Nyarlathotep... So much magic, knowledge, power at your disposal, and you do what? Protect frail humans in your circle and make sweets day to day. You could be so much more."

He rose and slid closer to where I hazily hovered. "We could be so much more. Together we could rule the human realm. Easily."

I laughed. "Look, Zeus. You've been gone a long time. There's a lot more people and places, and none of them take kindly to outside rule. Besides, I don't want that, or you. So back up, asshole."

He let out a beleaguered sigh. "As you wish, Randy. We could be darkness and lightning tearing across this world, bending it to our will, but you have no drive."

"To be a dark, horrible god? Definitely not. To kick your ass back to Kadath? I've got plenty of drive to do that."

"Such a waste," he said, a condescending shake of his head making a few strands of his gray hair tumble across his furrowed forehead. "Alas, I have no other choice. I shall drain you, then eventually crack dear Mia and rip all the power from Nyarlathotep. I will return to my former glory, here and in other realms, and humans will remember why they fear storms."

"I've never been scared of a little thunder."

Zeus didn't reply. Instead, he shot those same blue slivers of light straight at my dream-walking form, wrapping it around me tight. I struggled, but I felt them burrowing deep and reaching back. Beyond. To where my physical body stood. Apparently he needed me there in the flesh, which he wasn't going to get.

DD swooped in, bolstered by my shadow power, and ripped the tendrils away from me, but Zeus wasn't deterred. He sent more and more, and we were locked in a weird magical stalemate for a few minutes, Zeus continuing to throw the same old fetching spell at me as if it would eventually work and DD and I ripping it off so it didn't have time to really do anything.

Tired of the redundancy, I finally slashed out with my spear, sending darkness toward the guy without any real idea what it could do. I wanted him to hurt, to stop, and that was the intention I put behind it. A thick darkness rippled in a wave across the space until it slammed into Zeus. He didn't buckle or fall or anything, but his eyes crinkled in strain and his lips thinned, which gave me a smug sort of satisfaction.

However, the issue was I wasn't real and didn't want to be real and solid there, because Zeus also wanted me in the flesh for some reason. I didn't know enough about my power to use it other than on instinct, so I was a little at a loss for what exactly I could do. I wanted to slash and hurt, and I was sure I could lash out in some way. I was unsure of the results, which made me temper my impulses a little bit.

I gathered DD to me and formed a bubble so Zeus would stop the fetching attack. I had no inky, power-filled Writhing like I'd had in Kadath and didn't know how to call it to the human realm, much less call or use it in some type of dream-walking form. What I did have was the same instinct I'd had at Mia's, the nose and taste for the magic Zeus poured out of him in his attacks. His fetching spell was dissipating, but not fast enough. I tasted it, and through me DD knew it, and it reached out to wrap around the blue streaks, which I suddenly somehow knew were a part of Zeus himself he had put behind the spell to give it form and power. I had DD squeeze harder and tighter, then yank back suddenly. Zeus stumbled for a moment as if I'd pulled on a rope tied to his waist. He didn't like that at all, if the rage in his now-glowing-gray eyes was anything to go by.

Zeus bared his teeth like a wild thing and yelled, "Enough!"

I smelled it first, the hit of ozone in the air, then saw the crackle of blue sparks across his knuckles a split second before he hit me with actual, honest-to-gods lightning. I should've seen it coming. He was freaking Zeus after all.

The charge hurt despite not having a body, causing my dream-walking form to convulse and buckle. I shook so hard, my hazy teeth clanked together in a vicious bite and I tasted blackened toast on my tongue. Struggling to get free of the electric streaks of power coursing all around me, I grabbed hold of the power he used against me, like I had the blue streaks of Zeus's spell, and for a split second, I saw flashes of highways merged and old buildings and dead grass shooting up through cracked sidewalks. Zeus yelled and shoved more power through the crackle, which resulted in my sliding back, back, back down whatever line brought me here. Whether he intended it or not, he'd expelled me from his apartment, back into my body, now crouched and heaving breaths on Mia's floor while she, Ny, and Rich hovered around me.

"What the hell?" Mia screamed, and I registered she was holding a phone to her ear.

I fell over, sprawling on my back and savoring the sensation of being back in my physical body. "What the god, more like." I passed out immediately after I got the last word out of my mouth.

# Eight

I opened my eyes to darkness. Not my type of darkness or shadow, but the darkness created by being squished face first against a black leather jacket. I breathed deep, getting a big nose full of musk and magic. Combined with the zing washing over my senses, grounding me, I knew it was Ny, and I breathed deep to get more of him.

He could tell I was awake and moved, so I sat at arms-length. I smiled up at him, which is when I noticed the deep, dark swirling void of his eyes and the scowl on his face. "What the fuck were you thinking, Randy?" he yelled.

I reeled back, from the power rushing out of him and his tone. He'd never yelled, not that I'd heard in our months together. Definitely had never yelled at me.

"I was thinking about saving my sister," I said as I wiggled out of his grasp and sat up on my own. I was still firmly seated on the floor, so I did my best to crawl to my feet with some dignity. My best wasn't great, but I managed to come to standing so I could square off with a seething Prince. I didn't get the chance to say more to him, because Mia shouldered her way between us, her anger matching Ny's, her petite body shaking as she jabbed a finger hard in my chest.

"I don't need you saving me. Not like that, at least. Not with any stupid, headstrong, run in-with-guns-blaz- ing-and-no-thought-about-consequences type bullshit. Oh, and I talked to Merry by the way. Expect a lecture from her later too." Of course she'd told Merry on me, the snitch.

I went back a half step and rubbed the small point on my chest where she'd dug in a little too hard. "First off, ouch. Watch your pointy little finger. Second, I did what needed to be done."

"No," Ny said, staring from behind Mia, boring into me with all-black eyes, no sparkle of space or sky to be found. "You reacted, and reacted badly. You didn't speak to anyone, tell us what you felt, thought, or planned. Did not even plan. There were other ways we could have helped Mia. Together and without the same level of danger."

"How was I supposed to know that?"

"By talking to me!" Ny roared, the sound as loud as any he'd made in his lion form, rattling the windows and walls. Everyone else in the room flinched.

I stared, shocked into silence, and Rich stepped up like he was about to add in his own two cents too. I wasn't about to take anything from him—I barely knew the guy—so I cut him a do-not-mess-with-me side eye, and he backed away quickly, dropping his hands and whatever he was about to add to the pile-on-Randy moment. DD hovered, whole and well, still and silent down the line, and I sensed it agreed with all of them. The traitor.

"Sis, you did what I did. And look where it got me," Mia said, her eyes glassy and vague, her voice still hoarse from her ordeal minutes ago.

Her words made my mind do a record scratch. Jumping in headfirst was what I was prone to do. What all us Carter sisters were prone to do when one of us was in trouble. Our enemies had been hurt by it, sure, but they had used it to their advantage too many times now.

It'd also made us do harm to ourselves, and not just regular old harm. Life-changing harm, especially in the case of Mia.

To top it all off, I myself knew what I'd done was impulsive and stupid. It was driven by rage and a need to lash out, not by any type of thought or strategy, which meant once I ended up in front of Zeus, I'd had to keep reacting, keep guessing at what to do. I'd had no plan, no mooring, no idea what was happening or why. It was reckless and impulsive and could have ended so much worse than it had.

My shoulders shagged as my chest deflated along with my anger. "I know. I can't really say anything to justify what I did. I was scared for Mia and reacted without thinking."

Ny stepped around my sister and pushed into me, leaning his forehead down to rest on mine. He was breathing heavy, as if worry and anger made him breathless. "I was terrified for you, sweetling." His eyes blinked closed before he pushed back enough to snare my gaze. I was happy to see small specks of stars begin to blink back into his eyes, even if his voice took on that weird imperious echoey quality it sometimes had when he said, "You must promise me you will never do anything similar again."

I bristled at the command of it, but I also understood where it came from, so I bent a little for him. I reached a hand up to cup his cheek, his face rubbing against my hand like the feline he was, and said, "I promise to try."

He stilled, his nebulous gaze sparking as he thought about what I was offering: a commitment to attempt to do better, even if I couldn't always do better. A curt nod was all I got in return, but he gave a quick kiss to my wrist too, and the zap of energy from his touch skittered across my skin in the usual, delightful way.

"Do or do no—"

"No need for Yoda quotes, Mia. I get it. I do. I only say try because I can't fully guarantee I'll never do it again, because we all know how I can be sometimes, and at those times I'm usually not thinking too deep on past promises. I can guarantee I'll work to do better in the future."

My sister wiggled between me and Ny, literally pushing the Prince of the Dreamlands, the Crawling Chaos, out of the way like he was nothing. Rich's eyes bugged out, and he took a step closer, like he'd have to defend her, but I knew he wouldn't.

Ny smirked, stepped back, and waved an arm gallantly at my sister. "By all means, Mia. Please do see to your sister."

Mia harrumphed at him, and Rich looked between me and Mia and Ny for a moment, his mouth slightly opened in shock, his head shaking at what he'd just witnessed.

Ny went over and stood by him, arms crossed. "The Carter sisters are a force unto themselves, my friend. Do try to act less surprised in the future."

Mia hugged me after rolling her big brown eyes at the Outer God. No fear, no remorse, and my heart fluttered at it all. At the power and sheer will my sister had, and the love I had for her. At the love I had for the Prince and he for me, to take such sass. It was its own form of magic, and one I wanted more of in the future. A form of magic worth protecting, though I did need to be smarter about how I went about protecting all of it.

WE'D ALL CALMED ENOUGH to sit our butts down and talk about what had happened. First, Mia explained her experience. She and Rich had been having a mellow morning, planning on where and how to start their Necronomicon research, when she'd been hit by a boat load of magic. Her words exactly. She couldn't tell how long she was under attack—Rich said about ten minutes or so total—but did know a few things: someone was trying to pull her somewhere else, the book recognized it right away, and they both dug their heels in, figuratively and literally, so they couldn't be taken.

"Has the book shielded you prior to this, Mia?" Ny asked.

"Yes. When we were in the Dreamlands. It sometimes helped me mentally handle things there." She squirmed a bit at the answer, like she didn't want to fully say.

"Very well," Ny said, abandoning the line of questioning for the moment. He turned to me. "Now on to your adventure," he said. The words were flippant, but his voice was hard. He didn't yell again, but he was clearly unhappy about what I'd done. It'd take time for him to forget it, I knew, so I plowed ahead with my story.

I described Zeus, the apartment somewhere in downtown Columbus, and his attempt to tempt me over to the dark side. When I got to the mages, Mia let out a gasp of surprise. "No way!" she yelled. "Are you sure they were the same dudes?"

"Yep," I answered with a pop. "Zeus even said as much. Told me all that's happened since then was because they spotted me in the restaurant."

I wanted to shove the guilt aside, but it was piling up hard and fast, threatening to take over and wall up any other emotion. My breath was shaky. So was my hand when I felt Ny take it.

"What Zeus has done was planned for millennia, Randy. There is no other way he could have accomplished it. He used you as a pawn in a larger scheme."

"Besides," Mia said. "He's the one doing all this shit. Not you. It's not on you, sis."

I wanted to believe that, but logically thinking something and feeling something were two different skills, and I'd never quite mastered the art of matching them up. The guilt over Deb's death, Mia's new crap, Merry having to play hallway monitor in my head, Gareth getting sucked into a void thing and possibly changing. All of it felt on me somehow.

"She is right, sweetling. Even if you cannot believe it now, you must try to push past your guilt so you can do what is required."

That I could do. It was the buoy I needed to cling to so I wouldn't get drowned by the waves of guilt I felt. I needed to act, and I could shove the rest aside until Zeus was permanently out of the picture.

I continued my story, talking more about my instincts and the smell and taste of Zeus's spells. Even his magic, because it wasn't until I retold what happened that I realized I could taste his lightning magic before he'd used it, like I could other magic and spells.

Ny nodded, his brow creased in thought. "You have Hecate's power, Randy. Which means you should be able to identify spells. Apparently through taste. What you can then do with them is a different issue altogether."

"Is this something you can help with?" I asked.

"I can help with your growing shadow and darkness powers. I can help you with natural magics. I cannot help you dissect or understand your spellcraft powers. I know some spells, such as astral projection. Which, by the way, is what you did today without any effort whatsoever. Truly remarkable, really. However, beyond basic spells and sorcery, things I learned from Hecate eons ago, I know little of spells. I do not require them to hold or use my natural power. You need someone who knows more spell magic. Someone well versed in spellcraft theory and casting."

"Good thing we have someone like that practically in the family," Mia said before I could reply.

Looked like it was back to Harley's mage lair for more talk about spells and what I might be able to do with or to them. I needed to chat with Merry anyway, about Warm Regards business and an idea I'd had about the weird flashes of places I'd seen when Zeus zapped me. Best do both at once and try to get as much sorted as possible.

Which brought me back to the weird vision flashes I'd gotten from Zeus. I asked Ny what they were, but he had no concrete answers. "I did not see them, so I cannot say," he told me. More than a bit frustrating.

"Can you at least guess if they were real or not? Was I seeing an actual place here that could be important?"

He gave a shrug. "As I already said, sweetling, I cannot say. You are the only judge of this. Did it feel real, conjured, or forced?"

I took several beats to think about it. Closed my eyes and brought my mind back to the flashes of images and snippets of detail in them. "My brain says they're real places, but I can't be certain they're important."

"If they came from Zeus, they're important," Rich said, and Mia muttered her agreement at his side.

"Well then. Best dig into those details and see what we might be able to suss out about his future plans."

"Very well, Randy. Any other questions or topics of discussion before we depart?"

He'd asked the room, but I jumped in with one final but important question. "One more thing, Ny. How do we kill a god?"

# NINE

The question, obviously, had gone unanswered. If Ny could answer questions about the death of gods with the Book of Knowing, he'd have known when and how Hecate was killed and would've probably already taken out Zeus. Now, without the Book of Knowing in his corner and no access to any other source we knew of that could possibly provide clear directions for god slaying, we didn't have an easy answer. Not like I was expecting one or anything, but it would have been nice for things to be wrapped up neatly and quickly. Unlikely, but nice.

More research was on deck for all of us, but more training was my priority. Which meant I was off to see Harley bright and early the next day.

When she swung the door to her condo open, I shoved a platter of cinnamon blondies in her face before she could even say anything. "Here. Payment for help and whatnot."

She chuckled, taking the platter from me and turning to step into the darkened interior of her house. She threw over her shoulder "I usually charge more than this."

"Yeah. I could guess from the condo, Harley. I thought I'd get a family discount though." I shut the door after myself and scurried behind her long, trouser-clad stride up the stairs.

Harley bypassed the library door and continued down the hall, turning a corner and heading for what I now knew was the kitchen-living room combo overlooking High Street. Not my quieter, older section of Old North High Street but the bustling and trendy Short North section of the city-long avenue.

I knew why we'd detoured here first when I heard my sister Merry's voice chime out, "Hey, love. Hey, sis." The sweetness of my sister's looks was rivaled only by the sweetness of her nature, and I loved her for it. She'd chewed me up one side and down the other last night over the phone for the stunt I pulled at Mia's yesterday. No one would know it today though, by the genuine smile on her face when she saw me walk into the room.

Harley didn't reply to her chirped greeting. She deposited the platter of treats on the large island in the middle of the kitchen and moved to my sister, who was working on an Excel file on her laptop. Merry lifted her head straight up to look into Harley's face with a wide, sappy grin. Harley gave a smirk back and dipped a few inches to kiss her forehead, her dark face and short-cropped coiled curls skimming to the side of my sister's head to whisper something in her ear that made a giggle bubble up and a blush creep across her cheeks.

"You two are freaking adorable," I said, taking a seat beside my sister and leaning into her. I rested on her shoulder to shoulder, so she took some of my weight and I took hers in turn.

I almost slipped from the barstool when Merry yelled, "Oh, blondies!" and reached over for the platter, shoving her laptop over with one hand as she brought the plate to sit in front of us with the other. "A solid midmorning snack."

"I thought so. Harley didn't appreciate them much," I said, adding a little pout in for effect.

Harley stood, leaning against the counter on the other side of my sister and facing me. "I didn't say that. I said I usually charge more for my services."

Merry spun toward her with narrowed eyes. "You're not charging Randy, are you?"

She cocked her head and simply stared at my sister, the light of day and the odd glow of her sigil tattoos bouncing around her face to make her smooth brown skin practically shimmer.

"Of course not," Merry huffed, as if Harley had answered her question out loud. She passed out napkins and blondies and poured me a big cup of coffee in a bright-pink mug with the phrase "unicorn juice" scrawled across it in holographic rainbow script. She took a big bite of her own tasty treat and waited until after I swallowed my first gulp of coffee to ask, "You going to tell us everything that happened yesterday?"

She knew the basics from Mia and her yell-fest at me last night, but she knew there was more to it. Merry had felt it. When I dream walked, she got my feelings down our magically implanted connection thanks to a different Harley spell, and since astral projection was a heightened form of dream walking, she'd been frantic. I'd spent a good deal of time being told off by the middle Carter sister directly after getting told off by Ny and Mia. Thankfully Gareth and Harley had given me a break. I don't think they did it because they weren't worried or pissed. They both knew whatever it was they'd lecture me about had probably already been covered by everyone else.

"Sure," I said around another bite of moist, cinnamon goodness. I tried to catch some wayward crumbs with my hand, but failed, before I went on. I told the duo everything, paying particular attention to the spell stuff because of Harley and the vision stuff because of Merry.

Harley knew what was important for her to know and why. When I'd asked to meet up with them both at her place, I'd already mentioned I needed some extra spellcraft training because of the Hecate power business. Merry, on the other hand, needed more explanation.

"Merry? Do you think you could find old abandoned or for-sale property if I gave you some basic descriptions?"

"Possibly. You talking about the vision things you got from Zeus?"

"Yeah. I think they're real places here, and I can't be certain, but I also think they'll be important to whatever his next plan of attack is. We need some way to get the upper hand, and finding out locations could be it."

"Okay. Tell me everything you can remember from your flashes or whatever. I'll see what I can find in business records and with Google Maps. I also have a friend in commercial real estate. I'll contact him and see if he knows of anything."

"Good, good," I said. I recounted everything I saw in those odd flashes from Zeus as Merry took notes. Finally done with the fight blow-by-blow, vision descriptions, and fabulously good blondie-coffee combo, I wiped my mouth with my napkin and slapped one hand on the table, clanking the novelty mug down with the other hand. "On a less end-of-the-world-as-we-know-it note and more of a personal note, any word on progress at Warm Regards?"

Harley, surprisingly, jumped in with the answer. "The inspections are done. I smoothed those over for you. Also found you a contractor who can do the work ASAP. You'll need to meet with him Friday morning. Hope that works. Three days should be long enough lead in for contractor talks."

"I'm fine with it. Thanks, by the way. You didn't have to step in and help with this."

Harley hit me with her hard brown eyes and said, "Didn't have to, wanted to, just like I want to help you with spellcraft."

"Nice segue." I stood from my stool and gave Merry a quick hug. "See you later, Merry Berry. Duty calls."

"Have fun doing your magical-lady things," she called to our backs. Her bright, cheerful hum followed us out of the kitchen and down the hall.

IN HER COOL, BLUNT manner, Harley got right to business. She waved a hand at me to sit as she herself leaned, hands in trouser pockets, her tan-on-tan look today doing more to highlight her gorgeous dark skin and the sigil tattoos on her toned forearms. "I assumed, once things settled, you'd come asking about Hecate."

I snorted. "I didn't. Feels like I ask you too much as it is."

Harley shook her head. "Look, you know me. I'd be the first to tell you to talk to someone else if I wasn't invested, partly because you're my friend, partly because Merry loves you, and partly because it now comes down to Hecate."

"This is something you know about?"

She gave a shrug then, moving to pace the length of the short wall lined with bookcases. "As mages are all about magic and spells, Hecate is a big figure in our field. All of it is theoretical, obviously, because no person in living memory has ever interacted with the goddess, but plenty of mages believe Hecate was the first actual mage, or the first thing to use a spell, and that she actively passed the knowledge she created down to humans."

"Ny told me she taught him spells," I said, supporting the theory Harley was laying out.

She paused. Froze more like it. Then closed her eyes. "Fuck. Of course the Prince would have known her. I must be slipping."

"We've had a lot of shit going on, Harley."

"Truth." She shook the thoughts off and started back up with Hecate.

I folded my legs crisscross under me in the overstuffed armchair and gave her my full attention.

"We have Nyarlathotep to confirm some of this, and I'll be having a talk with the guy soon, but this is what many mages believe. What I believe. Long ago, Hecate developed spellcraft and passed it down to humans. First women, then men. Some historical fragments support the idea, but nothing beyond a few scattered ancient texts. Hecate disappeared from magical memory long ago, lending credence to the death theory from Ny."

"Hecate was some feminist giver goddess then?"

"In some ways. She was likely a regular goddess in other ways too, ways not great for humans around her."

"In all this theoretical talk of Hecate, or any god of Earth actually, is there any word on a god or goddess's power being transferred to a human?"

She looked genuinely sorry when she said what I knew she'd say. "No, Randy. No records or histories I've ever read, and I've read a lot, have ever mentioned such a thing. I'd say it was impossible, but..." She stopped pacing to wave her hands in my direction.

She moved closer, her head cocked in her studied way and her dark eyes whirling with thought. She stopped in front of me, leaning slightly into my space as if trying to better see something hovering around me. DD was there hopping around as per usual, but she'd been around it enough to not be concerned with its hyperactivity. Something else drew her attention. "Randy, do you realize power washes out of you in waves now?"

"What do you mean?" I felt it, sure. The jump in power, the now constant and deeper thrum of my magic inside me.

"DD flocking to you was the thing marking you the first day I saw you. Now, it's pure magic and power. It's a constant shadow and darkness rolling off you, as if it were created by you."

"Sorry," I muttered.

"No. I don't mean it's a bad thing. It's all good, Randy. It's simply a different state of being. You know you unlocked Hecate's power inside you when you went to the other place and used the silver key."

Instinctively, I rubbed the silver key now dangling from a black leather cord around my neck. I wasn't sure I'd need it again, but when a bony Outer God's servant says to keep something, it might be important, so I'd wanted to keep it close. I'd worn it there, tucked tight and safe under my clothes, since returning from the Dreamlands.

"You also have more connections to spells now. You can taste and smell them?"

I nodded and she went on.

"Okay. This gives us something to work with."

She went back to the books and pulled an old, brown leather-bound one down and handed it to me. "Not many mages can both do and undo spells, but it is a skill some have acquired. This book discusses it at length, so read it."

I turned the heavy thing over in my hand and inwardly groaned at the additional homework. "Fine, but can you help me with some hands-on practice?"

"I'm not able to undo spells with pure power. I know a few counter-spells which work to undo other, very specific spells, but that's all I got." She shot a cocky grin at me and straightened as she continued. "It's irrelevant. I know my shit, and I can help you work through the theory until we get it down in practice."

If anyone could, Harley could, so I followed her to the training side of the room to start my spellcraft lessons, dragging the book along with me.

# Ten

"Spellcraft is different from spells," Harley said as she moved me to the far end of her training space. She paced back about fifteen feet and turned to face me again before she continued. "Magic is a natural occurrence, but spells are created by someone or something. Magic is used to charge spells, and only certain humans can access magic and, therefore, use spells to change or manipulate the natural world. You know all this. Spellcraft, however, is a niche subset of harnessing magic. It is the specific act of doing and undoing spells. Creating spells is a unique talent amongst master mages, but the skill has been around and written about for centuries, so even mages who do not have the talent at least know a thing or two about it in theory. Destroying spells is a much trickier and more unusual gift altogether. In fact, it's a gift no living mage has, at least no mage I know of, and I know plenty. Also, one few have written about in the past, which leaves us with few research options."

"What I did with Mia, it was undoing a spell, right? Something my Hecate power somehow allows me to now do?"

"Yes, and it does have direct correlation with Hecate, but don't get it twisted. What you actually did to Mia was no gift in and of itself. You were both lucky it saved her, but it wasn't spellcraft. It was reckless and stupid. You had no thought of what it could have done to her or any idea what the spell actually was. It was all guesswork on your part. It ended well this time. Another time you could have accidentally ripped your sister to shreds, body and soul, trying to pry a spell away from her without thinking through what the spell could do to her when she was in its thrall." She said it with no malice. It was fact for Harley, which somehow hurt even worse.

"I know. I know. Won't be doing it again."

"You will undo again, only the next time you do it, you'll do it with intention."

"The backbone of all magic," I said, more than a little grumbly about the put-down still.

"Exactly. You run off half-cocked. You react instead of act and don't put proper intention into your magic. With your power and range, lack of clear intention could be disastrous for you and anyone around you. You have to control your magic, not let it control you."

I breathed deep and nodded. I agreed with what she said, but it had been hard to remember when my little sister was twisting on the ground in silent agony. "All reasons why I'm here right now."

Harley wasn't one to nag about a point already made, so she went for a more practical approach. "Draw a ward of protection around the space you're in, using the simple ward spell I first gave you."

Easy enough. I'd done it to Warm Regards, and it wasn't much help there, so I figured this was more for demonstration than necessity.

After I focused on the ward circling me and DD, and my power and intention snapped it into place without having to draw a single sigil, I said, "Done."

Harley glowed slightly, a half-hidden sigil on the inner wrist of her left hand flaring a millisecond before I smelled and tasted cloves mixed with ground stone. Then I saw it, a crack of something purplish gray ramming into my ward, burrowing a hole into it, and shattering it around me like a baseball sailing through a window.

"How'd you do that so quickly?" I asked, still rolling the taste of her spell around in my mouth.

"I gave you the spell. It's one I know inside and out. While I can't crack open all spells, I can splinter any spell I know well enough. I'm one of the few who've mastered that particular counter-spell."

"Because you knew it you could take it apart."

"Yes, because I know a specific ward-breaking spell. My power ends with my knowledge, meaning I can't just poof spells out of existence on a whim. You, however, seem to have the ability to learn a spell by smell and taste, parcel out what's needed to rip it away or crack it, and then use your power to do so. It's almost as if you're a master key to any magical lock."

I instinctively went to rub the silver key around my neck once again, thinking Harley's metaphor was more than accurate. Unlocking Hecate gave me the power to unlock any spell.

Harley stepped closer. "There might be more. Being able to track back to Zeus was spell dissection and reuse. I think, just maybe, you'll not only be able to dissect spells and take them apart, but also put the components back together again. At least, once you become better at recognizing the flavor of certain spell components. Let's test it."

For the next thirty minutes, Harley threw out spells. All had an uncurrent of clove, which seemed to be the special something Harley added to every single spell. Beyond the clove, every hit had a unique smell and taste, something I could roll around my mouth and come to recognize. Her flame spell tasted like ash; her shield spell tasted like stainless steel. The wind she used to whip around DD, to its delight—if its little bouncy dance was anything to go by— tasted like a spring day. When she threw a blast of power at the wall so strong it crumbled the drywall in a spidery circular pattern, my mouth filled with a bitter, earthy taste. After each spell, she asked me to describe my sense of it, recite it back and explain why I thought those particular tastes matched the specific spells.

Once we started talking it all out, it came easier. I was a baker, after all. I was used to learning through trial and error when it came to taste and flavor combinations. Which might be why my now-natural magic-detecting system was centered in smell and taste more than anything else. Those were the senses I'd honed over years in the kitchen.

"Let's give something new a try." Harley moved farther away, almost all the way back toward the library area.

"Scared?" I asked with a smirk.

"More like cautious," she replied when she faced me once again. "Now, take a few of the magic tastes, remember them, and try to put them together in your mind. Meld them so you create something new. And don't forget the intention component. As you connect them, think clearly of what they could create together and envision it. Not only envision it, but turn your mind to it as an end goal."

I closed my eyes to better focus. I picked the two of the tastes most recognizable to me: ash and steel. Dealt with those enough being around flame and cooking, so I went with those. It meant I was working with a flame spell and a shield spell. It seemed logical enough to combine into a flaming shield. I didn't really know if it was a thing, but I was determined to give it a try. I thought of it, a thick wall of flame that could close me off, protect me.

I pushed DD away as best as I could, though it still hovered behind me, ready to swoop in if needed. Much like me and my sisters, we seemed to be in a constant game of who was protecting who at any given moment.

"Give me space," I mentally told DD down our line, and it hovered a few more feet back, but only a few. Looked like it was all I was going to get, so I let it be and focused back on the task at hand.

I pulled the memory of the tastes and smells of each spell back to mind, placed them on my tongue in a way, and rolled them around to identify each nuance. I thought of what I wanted, set my mind to create it with the thrum of magic in my body that was growing more insistent. The bass beat in my gut cranked up, taste flooded my mind, and I saw black for a flash before orange and yellow filled my vision. A wall of flame materialized inches in front of my face, to be exact, and it was hot as hell too.

I stumbled back, falling to my butt just as DD swooped in to create a stretched shield of itself between me and the giant wall of flame licking from floor to ceiling in Harley's place. There were even growing black scorch marks to go with it.

"Shit, shit, shit," I said to myself as I scrambled up to standing.

Harley yelled from the other side of the hot-ass wall I created, "Undo it! Take it apart! Now!"

I concentrated again, took the tastes I blended in my mouth, and tongued them apart, making them distinct. Then I pushed them back and away, as if they were nothing. I thought about them being singular and nothing. A contradiction, but it worked. The wall wavered, sputtered, and disappeared. I might not have believed it had even been there, except for the heat still stinging my face, the scorch marks scarring Harley's pretty wooden floors, and the still-beating thump of full-tilt magic coursing through my guts.

"Sorry," I said, as Harley stalked up to me.

She didn't seem to hear it. Her eyes were wide with something else. "Fucking spectacular," she said, taking me in her arms and giving a whoop as she spun my body around.

It was so out of Harley's usual stoic manner, I was startled into laughter. She set me down. "I've never seen someone do such a thing. Hot damn. I need to think about this more."

She seemed to be talking to herself more than me as she strode purposefully back to her library shelves and searched for a particular book.

"Does this mean we're done?" I asked as I followed.

She turned to look me up and down. "Yes. For now. I need to think about the implications and next steps. I need to read. You, however, need to practice on your own." She paused. "It might be better if you practice on not-so-dangerous spells."

I barked out a laugh. "You think? I'm staying with Ny right now. He might not be as happy about scorch marks on his floors as you apparently are."

She gave me her full attention for a moment. "Good point. In fact, using Gareth and Ny to help you practice may be for the best. Gareth can provide you with new, less destructive spells to work with, and Ny can possibly help you discover more dormant Hecate powers beyond the instinctual spellcrafting."

"Gotcha," I said, moving toward the door, thinking about saying bye to Merry before I left the condo for Ny's place again.

"Randy," Harley called. When I looked back at her over my shoulder, she was standing tall, her tan shirt and trousers impeccable as ever, her arms crossed so her sigils glowed against the fabric at her chest, her eyes thoughtful and all on me.

"I know you still have questions about why you have these powers and what all you can do with them. I'd have the same damn questions if I were in your shoes. I'm sorry I can't answer them for you. I'm more sorry to say you may never find good answers. What I'm not sorry about is that it's you who has these powers."

When I looked at her confused, she sighed like I should already know this. "You're you, Randy. Caring, fiercely loyal and protective, conscientious... Not all people have those traits. What I just witnessed was an awesome level of power, which if handed to the wrong person, could be very dangerous. It's why you need to curb your impulses more. The same loyalty and protectiveness that makes you a person who could wield power without overusing it could also make you blind to the consequences of overdoing it when someone you love is on the line. It might be your most godlike trait, so don't be like them. Think before you do."

I took in what she'd said, the good and the bad, and gave her a wave in reply. What could I say? She was right. I was too impulsive for my own good and didn't always think through the direct consequences of my actions when I had big emotions. Hopefully, the good Harley saw in me, and I believed was in me myself, would balance it out. Along with some shoves in the right direction by people who could help me think before I did, to maybe do a little better than a god.

# Eleven

Gareth was happy to help with spells, and he showed me a sweeter side of magic as he did. He'd been helping with Nate, mostly discussing magic and answering questions up to this point, but the mentor role was suiting him well. Just like I'd thought it would.

I needed a little lesson in magic too, and not because of my Hecate powers. I'd been in survival mode with all my magic for months. I'd done cool-as-hell things, for sure. I'd traveled to different realms and moved through shadows and conjured things out of thin air. Still, all of it had been done in reaction. Defense. I hadn't had the time or space to learn spells without a focus on fighting or defense. It was practical, but it made magic a little harsh in my mind.

After we worked with a few unfamiliar ward and repelling spells for about thirty minutes in Ny's backyard, Gareth sat me down at the small wrought iron table. His big hands firmly squeezed my shoulders as he leaned down from behind me. His breath was a sweet breeze ruffling my messy bun when he whispered, "Close your eyes, Randy."

I felt a tingle on my skin before I tasted the distinct taste of Gareth's sweet magic musk mixed with a floral note. Not just any flower, but tulips, which were long past blooming stage. My eyes popped open, and there, in Gareth's palm, was a tiny mound of dirt with a perfectly formed red tulip sprouting right in the middle.

"What the what?" I breathed, awed by this new magic.

Gareth smiled wide before he said, "Shhh. Don't tell Ny. He might not like the fact I plucked up one of his tulip bulbs."

"Not an issue," the Prince purred from behind Gareth, where he leaned against the side of his house like he'd been there the whole time.

I was too distracted by the wonder of what I saw, the twist it brought to my chest, to pay attention to him popping up out of nowhere. "You can grow things with magic."

"Of course," Gareth said, his tone gentle.

"Magic is good in a fight, sweetling. It is also a tool of creation. A force for change that is not always violent or reactive," Ny said as he moved up onto the small patio.

Gareth moved to place the tulip in the ground, a small sigil on his forearm flaring to life as he placed it on the dirt. I watched, awestruck, as the roots took hold on its own, planting itself in the dark dirt, rooting itself safely and securely in Ny's tiny flower bed. I didn't even realize I was crying until his dirt-smudged hand came up to stroke my cheek, wiping my tear away.

"Randy?" he asked.

"It's just so beautiful," I said with a heavy breath, "and I always thought of magic as so hard."

"I think you forget our magic, Randy," Ny said.

I had, but not exactly. "The magic we make together is a lot of fun to make, but we've also always used it for other, not-so-fun things."

"True," Ny said, "but it is magic on par with what you just witnessed. It is an act of creation, not an act of destruction."

I nodded, understanding but still feeling the flower trick was something else, something new, something revealing about magic and its potential.

"Randy, you've been in defense mode for months, ever since you've started training in your magic. Even before that, for a long time, your magic was something dark and hidden. It makes sense, if you view magic as only based around fighting in some ways."

I shook off the shock and awe and tinge of sadness and wiped the tear, and bit of flower dirt, off my face. "A good thing to know. Now, let me try."

I closed my eyes, tasted the magic on my tongue, and unfurled the spell Gareth had used on the flower—also the earlier smaller spell he'd used when I wasn't paying attention, the one that had let him find the dormant tulip bulb in the ground. I studied their taste in my mouth, focused on how they felt there, then teased them out with my shadows, pushing it with intention.

Another red tulip shot up in rapid growth beside the newly re-planted one, a perfect little flower swaying from the force of its growth spurt. I clapped my hands together and maybe gave a small giggle of delight before moving over to see the little thing I'd created. DD hovered by it too, equally happy about this beautiful thing magic had brought into the world.

"I don't know why I never thought…" I whispered to myself, not finishing the sentence.

"Because you were never taught, sweetling. Which is on us all. Magic is fight and defense and power, true. It is also beauty and wonder. You've seen glimpses of it before, but for other ends. Let us see some more."

In a flash, the taste of darkness and space and raw power tripped across my tongue, and flowers sprung up all around the flower bed—tulips and daffodils and pansies making the brown earth bright and vibrant once again. A pruned rose bush unfurled, fat pink roses busting into full bloom in front of my eyes. It was magic, not in the sense I knew, but in the sense I remembered from long ago. Magic as fun and delight and happiness… the magic I'd known as a kid before I learned to be afraid of what magic could do. In my fear, I'd forgotten this part of it, even when I'd witnessed traces of it before.

The happiness, the connection between this new magic and the lovely magic we'd created together in the past, made my core flutter. I looked back at my guys. Gareth was standing in his feet-planted, arms-crossed-on-chest style. Ny lounged like a cat in one of the chairs, his eyes sparking at my joy.

I rose from the ground, moved to Gareth, and hugged him around his waist. Reaching up on my tiptoes, I kissed him softly. "Thank you," I said.

His face flushed, and his body stiffened in delicious ways.

"Do I not get a thank you as well?" Ny called from behind us.

"Wait your turn," I said, but I stepped around Gareth and moved toward him, stalking forward like he was prey.

His chair was pushed out from the table, but not enough for what I had in mind, so I gave his shoulder a playful shove. Taking my cue, Ny moved back. His hand shot out in a flash, hooked around my waist, and pulled me down to straddle his lap.

"A much better form of thanks," he muttered as he stared at my cleavage, which looked damn impressive in my tight V-neck tee. Without warning, he dipped down, raking his scratchy tongue up the center of my chest and back down, dipping deep into my cleavage.

I hissed out a breath and only faintly registered the taste of some type of ward going up around the yard. "Good looking out, big guy," I said between gasps as Ny placed hard, sucking kisses around my chest.

"Good man. I plan to make sweetling mewl loudly, and she might be embarrassed of it later," Ny said, his eyes full-on space as he looked up at me while speaking to Gareth.

I wasn't exactly inhibited before but knowing Gareth had put up a ward so no one could see or hear us, so we could still be out in the open, made me a little bolder. I shimmied my shirt up and off, leaving my white lace bra in place. Gareth had moved beside us at this point, and his groan of satisfaction at the mounds of my breasts on full display sent a shiver down my spine.

I looked up at him, saucy smirk in place, and tapped my lips with my pointer finger. He leaned down, taking my mouth in a deep, probing kiss. It was heavy, hot, a full-on assault on my mouth punctuated by Ny's hands roaming my breasts and belly and hips. I moaned into it, loving the feel of both of them on me. The moan turned into a gasp as Ny's hips angled upward, rubbing his now-obvious erection across my center.

I broke the kiss to focus on Ny. His head was thrown back, his eyes closed, his mouth opened in pure delight as I ground myself against him. He whipped back up and straightened in an impossible quick and smooth motion. His hand snaked between us and stopped at just the right spot in the crotch of my jeans, digging in with enough force to make me suck in a hard breath.

"Ride me, sweetling," he growled out, a question and demand somehow rolled into one. A quirk of his imperious godliness, I was sure.

I was too lost for words, so I stood on shaky legs and let him rise. I watched, mesmerized by the golden-brown sheen of the skin he exposed as he peeled his clothes off. I only snapped out of my stare when Ny whispered, "Your turn."

Gareth helped me undress then, his fingers lingering on my plump thighs, behind my knees, and the arch of my foot, and my body was a sizzling mass of lust driven by touch, sight, and even the taste of all our magic in the air.

I climbed back on the Outer God and wasted no time, rising on my knees so I could grab his heated erection in one hand as I lined myself up. I looked into Ny's nebula eyes and eased down, inch by tortuous inch, until we were both panting and gritting our teeth in feeling and frustration. Still for several beats, Ny eventually began to circle his hips from below, hitting the most delicious spots deep inside me without me even moving.

His hand moved to the back of my head, shaking my messy bun loose as he gripped me and brought me down so we were eye to eye. "I said ride me, Randy."

His voice was an echoing command I had no problem obeying, so I rose slightly on my knees. The bite of iron was harsh and thrilling in equal measure, and I paused in the air only a second before slamming back down.

I continued riding him for a few minutes, gasping with each luscious downslide, reveling in the groans and sparks of Ny's enjoyment. When I slowed a bit, I turned to look at Gareth, who stood a few feet away, leaning against the patio door, his dick straining the limits of his zipper as shallow pants pushed in and out of his half-open mouth. I called him over with the crook of my finger. He came, no hesitation. Ny saw my intent and his grip on my hips tightened, taking over the movement of our bodies so I could focus on the big guy.

I unzipped his jeans slowly and fished in his boxers to first cradle, then pull out his hot length. Gareth's taste was salty magic, quite literally, like a more concentrated, salinized version of his magical taste. It exploded across my tongue as Ny angled up in a new direction, hitting a spot deep inside, making me moan and shudder at the same time. I took Gareth deep, bobbing up and down on his hard length as best I could as Ny moved my hips back and forth at a punishing pace.

I heard the growl deep in Ny's throat, the shout of something in a language I didn't know, and he pulled me up slightly so I hovered a few inches above him. Then he dove in, over and over, until I ripped my mouth off of Gareth. I dug my fingers into Ny's shoulders and threw my head back as I screamed through my release. Ny's cries mixed with my own. As I calmed, I turned to Gareth, who was stroking himself, eyes fixed on where Ny and I were joined. I moved toward him, taking him in my mouth once more, redoubling my speed and effort, until a minute later he spilled down my throat, the magical taste of him all I knew for a few beats.

I hadn't been focused on anything but sensation and feeling for long minutes. Pleasure overrode everything, until I calmed my racing heart and looked around, saw the mix of my black shadows, Ny's space, and Gareth's greenish magic once again. I tasted the memory of the spell and our magic in my mouth, so it felt natural to gather our joined magic to me in a swirl around my right hand. I stared into it, thinking about how beautiful it was and for the first time about how beautiful magic could be in general, how it could and would be more than fighting and protection. How it was also care and growth and love.

I reached over to Gareth, gripping his forearm and infusing him with power like I'd seen Ny do so many times. It was part instinct, part new powers leveling up. Whatever it was, feeling the magic surge into the big guy felt like it fused an even stronger connection between the three of us, something I thought wasn't necessary or even possible. It felt natural and effortless, like breathing. Like flowers growing and blooming then returning to the earth.

"Impressive, Randy, but it might be a good idea to move this inside now," Ny said, his voice gruff from pleasure.

"Sure," I said softly, happiness and tiredness descending all at once. "Maybe you should carry me though."

Without any more encouragement, Gareth scooped me up in his big arms, warmth lightening his hazel eyes. "I have you," he said. He did. We had each other, and it was maybe the most beautiful bit of magic, even if I hadn't realized it before.

# Twelve

Friday came pretty quick. I was focusing all my energy on honing my ability to undo and remake spells. Gareth trained with me daily, helping me get better and faster at my spellcraft through basic repetition. I was doing and undoing spells like a fiend. It also helped Gareth. He was super busy with work at OSU, helping me, and teaching Nate on the side, but he shined when he was teaching. It gave him the drive we'd talked of, something his and his alone, a purpose he needed to fill up the part he called empty inside himself. I was more than happy to see it for my big guy.

As for me, I felt useful and in control for the first time in a long time. Bonus: any new spell I worked and unworked could give us yet another leg up we might have when going against Zeus. Who, by the way, had stayed quiet for a few days. He was lurking around somewhere, I knew. He was a dick who wouldn't just leave, so I knew he was out there planning something nefarious, as dickish god-type dudes so often did.

Like usual, good and bad things were swirling. One good thing this particular morning was the meeting with contractors at Warm Regards. Well, maybe not totally good, but it would be eventually. I was nervous to go in, see the space, and feel myself there, but my desire to have the creative part of me back and running free, the part of me not always focused on magic and fighting and power, was stronger than my fear.

I'd asked everyone else to stay away so I could have time in the space alone. No one protested too much, except DD, who stuck to me regardless of what I asked. I showed up for the contractor meeting with my literal shadow hovering and my sad, made-at-Ny's, regular old drip coffee in hand. Plus a big loaf of banana nut bread. Baked goods worked well as construction crew incentives. The contractor took my offering with a smile when I introduced myself. After I let us both in the cafe portion of my place, James sat with me at one of the cafe tables. We took a few minutes to chatter a few pleasantries, both of us obviously good born and bred Midwesterners, but I did appreciate it when James shifted to business rather quickly.

To my surprise, he had a lot done already. Schematics and everything. "Ms. Warren provided me with a good deal of information, and Ms. Carter let me in to see the back there a few days ago," James informed me. I guess Harley and Merry were much more on this than I'd even known. I'd assumed they lined up meetings and insurance payments and whatnot, which was enough for me to be thankful for, but they'd done more. I'd have to bring them something better than blondies next time I saw them.

We sat at the table, reviewing the plans, budget, and timeline James had already drawn up. I nodded like I understood the technical things when he went too in-depth. I did understand enough of what was there to see the outline of what he planned and how he and his crew would go about doing it. It'd basically be the same, just newer and a little more secure. All fine with me, including a price I thought fair for the work they'd have to do, so I signed off on it and gave him a check for the initial payment.

"Would you like to go over the space with me? Your sister showed me everything, and she and Ms. Warren explained the circumstances, but I'm happy to show you exactly what will happen."

I shook my head and thanked him for his time as I moved toward the door. It was a polite way to rush him out. I wanted to see the kitchen, the destruction still there, on my own. It was mainly why I didn't want anyone else with me. I needed to experience it by myself at least once so I could see if I could handle it on my own in the future.

I mean, traumatic shit happened in there, and thoughts of Deb still made my throat close and tears gather at the rim of my eye. I couldn't exactly bake tasty treats in a place I couldn't enter without a mini emotional breakdown. Figured a little exposure therapy on my own would help out the situation.

When I closed the front door and slid the lock into place, I took a moment to rest my forehead against the cool glass and focus on my breathing. In and out in deep, long spaces. DD, who'd been chill on my shoulder the entire time I'd chatted with James, zipped up to my temple and leaned there, the shadowy weight nearly insignificant but not. Never insignificant.

Using my palms to push myself straight, I whirled and stomped across the cafe, eating up the space as quickly as possible like a kid trying to get their veggies down so they could get to dessert. Only dessert wasn't waiting. Devastating memories were what was on the other side of the small doorway separating the cafe from the kitchen. I had to go, had to see what I could handle so I could start trying to handle more and more. Because I'd be damned if Wilbur was going to take the work and place I loved from me just like he'd taken my friend.

I burst into the kitchen all taut muscles and shaking hands, ready to fight. What I found was a relatively clean and clear space. The equipment that'd not been damaged was all unplugged and unsecured, shoved toward the back of the space, probably to give the crew room to work when they finally came in to do it. The now-open area of the kitchen appeared bigger than it should, a space unfamiliar in its emptiness. The floor was clean. No layers of rubble and dust to shift through like the last time I was there. The ragged edges of the wall were even smoothed, and the hole Wilbur had blown through had a duller edge than I remembered it having. When I inspected it more closely, I saw bolted plywood in the depths beyond the kitchen wall, secured to cover the hole in the outer brick someone had to create to make the gas leak story plausible. The pipes, wires, and other random junk inside a wall was sheared clean or rolled back. I skimmed the edges of the remaining drywall and felt it smooth to the touch. A different type of emotion hit my throat at the care someone took to make the space as clean as possible, to erase as many of the signs of disaster as they could.

I stepped back and my eyes hit the spot on the floor. There wasn't anything marking it. No chalk outline or blood splatter. Wilbur hadn't spilled Deb's blood when he'd killed her. He'd done it quickly and without mess. How could it even be possible, to take someone's life, their light, without leaving a physical trace behind?

My knees bent, my hands skimmed the smooth floor, and I didn't even realize tears were falling until I felt DD at my cheek, trying to skim the wetness away with its darkness. I nudged it to show appreciation for what it tried to do, but I didn't raise my hand. I let the tears fall. Deb deserved that. Shit, she'd deserved so much, and the weight of what she'd lost, what her family had lost, what I and everyone who knew her had lost, slammed into my chest so hard I almost toppled to the ground.

I held against the heaviness threatening to take me down, stayed crouched, tracing the space where her body landed. "I'm so damn sorry, Deb," I said into the empty space. I didn't know if there was a part of her somewhere who could hear it. I knew a lot more about gods now but not anything about what came after. I didn't know if I wanted to know.

Heaving myself up to standing felt like a chore with the weight holding me in place. I didn't try to shake it off or forget it. I let the magic thrum inside me work around it, weave into it. Like my magic, it was there and wasn't going anywhere anytime soon. Not without a lot of other shit happening to dislodge it.

The surprising thing is I could exist in the space, with the heaviness. I cried, but I didn't break down into a screaming, blubbering mess. The weight in my body shortened my breath, made my stomach churn, but I could move and think as I felt all of it. I could do it, be in Warm Regards. It was not fun. It hurt like hell, but it hurt in a way I knew would ease with every passing day, never leaving fully but becoming more and more integrated into who and what I was until it wasn't a part of me, but it was me whole and different. Like every piece of new magic I discovered or unlocked. The good and the bad and the sad and the happy were all mixing to make Randy Carter who Randy Carter was. It was not a good-time revelation, but there was a bit of comfort in it still.

I wiped imaginary dust from my hands. Whoever had cleaned here really had made it spotless. I gave one last look to where Deb died, or one last look for the day. I didn't know when I'd stop looking there, but it wouldn't be any time soon. Finally, I walked out, heavier and lighter at once, firm and soft, DD skimming my shoulder as I exited a place I'd once loved with all my being. A place I knew I'd find my way in again, with time, which wielded its own type of magic.

I KNEW SOMETHING WAS off right before I rounded the corner to the alley that led to my back parking lot. A brief whiff of ozone hit my nose and mouth right as DD went haywire. Not happy-excited shaking, but high-alert shaking a split second before it zipped in front of me and spread out into a shield.

I stumbled and I half yelled, "Jeez, DD, calm it down." Whatever else I might have griped about blanked when I got my bearings and raised my eyes to see those two Zeus mages standing in the alley, blocking my way.

"Shit," I muttered. I was in no mood for whatever bullshit they were about to pull, and I wished I could ignore them for a millisecond before I decided to be completely honest. "Look, dudes. I know you're working for Zeus or whatever, and we have a score to settle at some point because of that shit you pulled during the tornado, not to mention you're a couple of narcs who apparently helped get all this started. But I'm in no mood to play today, okay? Run along. For your own good."

The one I remember being the most vicious in his looks didn't step out of his pre-established role. He sneered at me, gave me an obvious look up and down as if I was crud on the alley floor, and rolled his shoulders as if ready to fight. The other one was smarter or more cautious, because he stepped back half a step as if he'd give me the space I wanted. The other one noticed the retreat and barked something at him in a language I didn't recognize. The words, whatever they were, were enough to stop his backtracking and force him to step up again. More the pity for him.

I felt the weight I'd settled minutes ago shift and swirl in me, turning in a flash into a churning, hot thing. The rage I knew would grow and black out everything else, but I couldn't let it happen. I needed to keep calm and in control. I chose to use snark to help me do it. "Okay.

Fine. You want to play it your way? Be idiots then. I have no problem taking you out now."

I commanded DD down my line, splitting it in two. Two DD shields at the mouths of the alley formed, hopefully blocking any sound or stray magic for random bystanders. I didn't want anyone hurt or stumbling on magic because these two decided to test me on a shitty day. I called down the spear, winking it into existence from the ether, pulling on its dark power. Why anyone would attack me in an alley, a place naturally filled with lots of shadows, was beyond stupid, but whatever. They did it and would learn the consequences. I took a few seconds to calm, to focus, and to think through what I could do to neutralize this myself rather than reacting to what they decided to throw my way, and a tiny inkling of a plan started forming in my mind, calming the hot churn in my chest the more I thought about it, centering myself.

When I focused back on the mages, the shittier of the two was swelling with swirling magic. He pushed down with open palms, sigils glowing from under the cuffs of his stark-white shirt and black suit jacket cuffs, shoving whatever he'd pulled back down toward his feet. The ground shook, and I smelled the essence of the Dreamlands and tasted a hint of rotted meat. My heart thudded harder, and the heat in my chest was shot through with ice water when I realized what he was trying to do. I didn't recognize the spell, but I knew what they'd likely done before. They were trying to once again summon one of the horror balls of death from the Dreamlands, those rolling masses of eyes and mouths and teeth. I'd last seen one in the witch house with Wilbur, but I wasn't packing heat like Gareth. They were definitely killable, but also terrifying, so no thanks.

I had to shut the shit down quick, and as the super-scowly one seemed to be the ringleader of all of it, he had to go. I reached out with the alley shadows, quickly curling them around and up his legs. He didn't immediately stop his spell, not until the shadows reached his waist and I made them squeeze. Maybe I squeezed a little too tightly, but I didn't really give a shit. I heard the crack of bones—multiple bones—right before he screamed and crumpled to the ground.

The spell he'd been performing sputtered and died without his sigils and intentions. Like Harley always said, intention was key, and it was hard as hell to hold onto magical intentions with broken bones.

I walked down the alleyway toward the duo. The scowly one yelled from the ground, pain and anger mixing in whatever words he shoved out into the other's face. The other, for his part, was trying to help his partner up, but he wasn't budging. He was firmly encased in shadow, held to the dirty floor of the alleyway as I stalked toward the two of them.

"I warned you I was in no mood for this today," I said, my face and words hard.

The scowly one shifted his face to me and bit out, "You do not deserve such power."

I shrugged a shoulder. "Deserve it or not, I got it and you don't. Whatever Zeus did to convince you to come at me here and now was stupid on both your parts. He should've known you'd fail, and you should've known you'd leave bleeding if you tested me."

The second one had scrambled back from me, his eyes wide and fearful, but he didn't move. He stayed as still as a rabbit caught in a trap, knowing there were few ways out of this. He gave the other a few calm words that sounded like warning, but the scowly one yelped in pain as he twisted around to yell back at him. The second, doing the first smart thing he'd likely done that day, ignored whatever the other dude said, scrambled to his feet, and hightailed it to the back of the alley. Sadly for him, DD was there and wasn't budging. He beat on it with frantic fists, but he wasn't going anywhere.

Ignoring him, I focused on the one at my feet. Even though I'd tamped down the heated anger inside, I could feel it flare here and there, especially when I thought back to all the shit people had done here, in my safe space... how they'd made it not safe for me and the people I loved. My vision flashed black for a moment and the guy froze, likely seeing my eyes do their new starry-night gig I'd yet to actually see myself. It had always seemed to happen when I was fighting and not, say, when I was around a mirror to check it out. No matter, it made the dude stop yelling in pain and demanding things in a language I didn't know. He froze, and fear crept over his face for the first time.

Tsk-tsking and shaking my head, I crouched at his side. "You should've been afraid before, buddy. It's a little late now."

With some impressive bravado—tempered by his clenched teeth and sputtering breath—he said, "You are no match for my master's power, so I have nothing to fear."

"I'd beg to differ, my dude. First off, I've survived fights against your master a few times now, which I think more than proves I can hold my own with the asshole." I leaned closer and looked left and right before I stared deep into the guy's eyes as I whispered, "Maybe more importantly for you in the here and now, your master isn't in this alley, is he?"

His bravado slipped, sweat forming a clear line on his forehead and upper lip. He gritted his teeth and waited, but I was done. Done with him and all the other assholes who'd tried to take me out. Who'd hurt those I loved. Who took and took and took wherever they were and never gave the world back a damn thing. Fuck them all. I was smart enough to know to truly be done, meaning I needed to do more than lash out in the moment. Thoughtful intention was key in getting the upper hand in magic, and for the first time, I had it without scrambling for it.

I was trying to be smarter. To act rather than react, as Harley would say. So I didn't ram the spear deep in his heart like I kind of wanted to do. Instead, I ripped it across his gut, spilling blood all over the belly of his pristine white button up.

# Thirteen

What I didn't fully understand was that blood smelled bad. Bile obviously smelled shitty, but the tang of blood wasn't exactly pleasant either, and as I hovered over the dude I'd literally gutted, both scents hit my sensitive nose at once. I managed to push down my wretch, but the shake of my spear-clutching hand and the sweat now forming along my scalp would've given me away if the dude had been watching me. He couldn't really focus too well on the outward physical signs of distress in another person when he was screaming in pain.

The other mage had stopped his pointless banging on DD and appeared a few feet from us. He didn't slide up immediately, not with me still holding my blood-dipped spear in my hands and my vision still hazed over in black as shadows billowed at my feet. Not brave enough for a confrontation with a wild-eyed kind of goddess.

When I acknowledged him, I jerked my head between the two. "If you don't get him out of here soon, he'll bleed out or piss me off more, neither of which would be great for his health right now."

I stood and took two big steps away from the bleeding mage, who'd replaced pain with hate in his eyes and was probably cursing me with his yells, though again I couldn't tell because he wasn't speaking English. I released my shadow hold on him and gestured with my spear for the other mage to gather his partner, flinging a line of blood in an arc across the alley. Grotesque and not at all cool, but effective.

The second mage gathered the man under his arms, managing to pull him up halfway. He looked behind him, checking his escape, and saw DD was no longer shielding the alley. I'd called it back. It zipped past the duo, pausing over them a moment before returning to me, landing right in front of my forehead, ready to protect if needed.

The mage looked back and forth a moment, trying to decide what to do, when I let out an exasperated sigh. "For crying out loud. You two have to be the most ridiculous henchmen of all time. Did you drive here or use magic to get here? Whatever you did, do it again before I change my mind about letting you go."

The guy nodded and dragged the dude out of the alley. The scowly one was still moaning and cursing. I suspect some of it was directed at his mage companion for the not-so-gentle tugging on his body. They rounded the corner, away from my lot and I suspect toward their escape: a car left idling on the side of the road. It wasn't even warded, which showed how stupid the two of them were. Anyone could've come up in the few minutes we fought and stolen their car. Luckily for them, and me, it wasn't.

I'd used my brains more than my spear, tucking a tiny bit of DD in the not-so-brave one's suit pocket, a small sliver of shadow he wouldn't feel or notice, but one I could use to track where they ended up. DD'd been a great scout in the Dreamlands, it was time to use it in the human realm to do more.

The remainder of DD bounced close, tense from the fight and having slightly divided attention because of the new mission. I gave it a comforting pat in my mind and moved down the alley, stepping over blood as I did. Before I exited, I flashed the spear out of existence, sending it back to the godly holding place, wherever it was.

My car had a pack of wet wipes in the glove compartment, and I'd never been more thankful for them. My hands shook as I wiped smears of mage blood from them. Once clean, I clenched them around the steering wheel to help stop the shake, touching my forehead to the leather there as I breathed deep, in and out, trying to calm all the bubbling and churning inside. I needed focus when DD gave me news, whatever it may be. Because wherever those mages went, Zeus was sure to follow.

I PULLED UP IN front of an abandoned storefront on the outskirts of Franklinton, a stone's throw from where the interstates and highways merged. It was one hell of a thing to navigate when traffic was bad. Luckily for me it hadn't been rush hour, so I sped over in my car, easing down the block where DD directed me about twenty minutes after the mages had left the alley.

The dated building was nondescript as hell. A sickly beige paint covered the old brickwork, the roof flat but apparently solid, and the banged-up door was barred with a metal cage. The same type of cage fit over the windows. Some of the window spaces were covered with plywood, a sure sign of missing glass. The ones still intact were covered up inside with what appeared to be dark furniture blankets. Weeds reached up in shoots through spidering cracks in the front stoop and sidewalk, large chunks crumbled or missing here and there. It looked like any abandoned or closed business in any depressed area of any Midwestern city. A little sad and rundown and a lot unremarkable. Probably a great place to do nefarious shit, as a god bent on world domination.

I recognized the building immediately. It'd been one of the flashes I'd seen in my weird vision from Zeus, so I knew we were in the right place. Add the fact DD had directed me here after the tiny part of itself couldn't get past the wards on the door the mages entered, and I was certain this was a place important to whatever Zeus was planning. What I wasn't sure of, and it was a big flashing red sign of uncertainty, was whether Zeus was inside the building right then.

"Ready for another quick solo mission?" I whispered out loud to DD, even though I could've just thought it. Talking to it was comforting sometimes, especially when I was nervous.

It jumped in my vision, its own little version of a yes, and I gave it silent instructions before it zipped away to do what I asked.

I stayed slightly hunched in my car, inching it forward so more of the front end and interior caught the shade of a much larger building. I'd parked across the street and a block down from my destination for a number of reasons, this being one of them. Less than ten seconds after getting its mission, DD popped back up by my side and a polite knock sounded on my shaded side window. Ny was always courteous about entering a space of mine.

I waved him in, and he opened the door, somehow smoothly gliding into the tiny front seat of my Mini Cooper with all his feline grace. His beautiful Egyptian nose was topped with a deep crease along his forehead and a frown marred his face as he whispered, "Blood." Of course he could smell it. Wet wipes were no match for Outer God senses. Before I could explain he asked, "Sweetling? Are you well?"

"About as well as I can be, seeing as I spent the morning mourning Deb, then was attacked by Zeus's mages before I gutted one like a fish."

His eyes, always night, flared with deep-space nebulas no human had ever seen. "Where are these mages now?"

I nodded at the abandoned building down the street. "Somewhere in there. Had DD follow them when I let them go so we could figure out some stuff about Zeus."

"Smart," he muttered, but his voice was rougher and deeper than the word warranted. He reached across the tiny space between our bodies and stroked my hair, digging his fingers into my scalp to grip me a moment before flexing his hand and letting it drop back. "You sent for me so we could investigate, yes?"

"Yep. Don't need to skulk around here on my own, and you were the one who could get here the quickest."

"I'll always be wherever you need me, whenever you need me, sweetling."

"I know." I gave him a quick, saucy smirk. "Or else I wouldn't have called."

It got little reaction from him, as he was apparently in no mood for teasing, so we moved on with recon. Ny was still better and quicker at shadow walking, which meant he was up for the first round of snooping. After a long minute, he popped back into the car and gave a general rundown of what he saw and sensed. The building was warded, but the wards weren't too complex and could probably be unspooled with my spellcraft. He saw one dingy, unblocked window in the back revealing a mostly empty rectangular space with a few tables and benches strewn about, sigils scattered around, and the two mages inside. One was tending to the other, who was still screaming and bleeding. He did not see or sense Zeus anywhere, or sense strong power coming from any single sigil, but he also felt a bit of resistance to his magical prodding, which could point to more advanced, and unknown, wards or spells lurking in or around the place.

I sat back in my seat and thought out loud. "Okay. Seems we have two options. The first is to get into the building, confront the mages again, and have a more solid look around the place to determine if or why it might be important to Zeus. The second is to do a little more recon, then bring all the info back to the others and think through a plan of attack."

"A thoughtful attack is always a good option, Randy. However, it runs the risk of our discovery of the space being detected. If Zeus senses we were here, he may well abandon this place and whatever plans he has for it. On the other hand, more time to plan gives us an advantage in any fight. We could also have Gareth, Rich, or Harley with us in a planned attack, which would be a significant advantage."

"All true," I muttered. I took a minute to think through my options in my head and nibbled on my bottom lip as I did. Ny reached over and pulled my lip from my teeth, his own mouth a shadow of his sexiest smile. I snorted out a laugh and shook my head to clear it.

"We need to go in," I finally said. "We can't risk him changing his plans, and the surprise could also give us an advantage. Maybe not as much as our own powerful mages and ghoul friend, but it'd still be good. Plus, if Zeus isn't here, there's the chance we can get in and out, find out more, and make sure he never learns we were here. Risky, but possibly worth it.."

"Both options hold risk, Randy. If you feel the risks of entry now are less than the risks of waiting, it is what we should do."

"I do," I said, my voice firmer and surer. "We start with shadow walking around the building so I get a feel of the wards, then we enter however we can, handle the mages in whatever way we need, and try to figure out what Zeus is doing with this place."

"Very well. Let us see what we can find."

"Wait," I said to Ny and turned toward DD at my side. I sent it a command down our line and felt it balk. "It's backup, DD. What we need. It's the best thing you can do for me right now," I said out loud. "Go."

DD jumped and jerked, showing its general unhappiness at its newest mission, before it blinked out. "I sent it to get Harley and Gareth. To lead them here," I explained to Ny.

"Excellent call," he said as he clasped my hand. "Shall we?"

"We shall," I confirmed.

"Come then. Sit on my lap."

"You charmer you," I said on a laugh, climbing over to inch into the shadow of the passenger seat with Ny.

"I do wish you were climbing on top of me for other reasons, sweetling. Alas, we have important things to do."

We did, for sure, but I still took a minute to grip close, sense the familiar power and heat of his body against mine, before we both began to fade, becoming one with the shadows.

# Fourteen

Shadow walking got easier and easier every time, especially with my growing use of Hecate's power. I moved side by side with Ny, using the shadows to coast around the building while also sending parts of them out to feel the perimeter and gather sensations. I worked my smell and taste, trying to ferret out what I could of the spells.

Ny and I didn't talk but moved together, a dark dance around the building. We stayed in the shadows for several minutes, gathering what info each of us could, before he signaled for me to stop and we materialized a few lots down, beneath the darker shade of an old tree.

"What did you sense?" he asked as soon as we were solid.

"A few spells here and there, a standard ward around the building, but nothing seemed too charged or solid for me to get through. I could taste them all, parcel out some components even at our speed. I think it'll be easy to break the wards and any protective spells inside. Maybe even easy to put them back if I take the time to really study each as I unravel."

Ny nodded. "There is no inherent magical source or power in the building, which means Zeus isn't here. He can surely cloak his power, but not well enough to fool us both. We'd still sense some trace."

"Good. So we continue? Break the outer ward, go in to snoop, and try to put it all back in place so Zeus doesn't suspect anything?"

Ny didn't answer. He simply walked forward, moving with some stealth through the light instead of shadow walking back. Stopping about ten yards from the side of the building with a beaten metal door, Ny waved toward the entrance. "Undo the ward and we enter here."

His voice held hints of command, which was Ny's way, and I couldn't exactly let it go. "Pretty please?" I replied, giving a saccharine-sweet smile and batting my eyelashes his way.

Ny offered a slight bow, which was enough for me to proceed. We had things to do, lairs to explore, and gods to root out after all.

The smell and the taste of the ward was vaguely familiar. I figured all wards had to have the same basic components because they all did the same basic thing: protect. This one had hints of bronze, an older metal of protection than the steel I'd tasted with Harley's or Gareth's warding or shields. It also held the burn of ozone, a sure sign of Zeus having a hand in it. Still, the tastes combined the same, and I easily teased out each ingredient, breaking it apart bit by bit in my mind, until the entire thing unraveled like cheap fast fashion. I left the bits alone, not gathering them to me to use again just yet. If we needed to recreate the exact ward, or close enough to it Zeus wouldn't notice, I'd need time and space to do that later. Now, we had to deal with what was going on inside.

Before we reached the door, I stopped Ny and whispered, "What do we do about the mages? We can't kill them, right? Dead bodies, or even blood without bodies, would give us away."

"Too true. I can handle the men. You concentrate on discovering more magic or spells once we're inside."

I was happy enough to let Ny handle it. The guys were assholes, but I wasn't exactly fond of killing people. I'd hurt one pretty damn bad already, and he might still die from the wound. If I could stop the killing blow now at least the human part of me might feel a little at ease about it.

We entered, Ny stepping through the door first, and soft music sounded in his wake. He suddenly held a shadowy, hazy flute in his hands. I stilled at the sound; it was unlike anything I'd ever heard. The notes seemed unreal, like living things traipsing across my skin, burrowing into my ears, and turning my mind toward other worldly thoughts and images. Before I was totally lost in the sounds, the thrum of my magic gave a loud, dissonant twang, a reverberation matching, then overtaking the energy of Ny's playing.

I shook my head clear and opened my eyes. I was clinging to Ny's shirt as both mages stood lazily swaying in front of him to a tune I could no longer hear. Even the one with the bleeding guts stood, though slightly hunched, his blood dripping onto the floor with each subtle movement.

"I was worried a moment," Ny said, turning to me.

"Oh, you almost Pied Piper'd me, for sure, but no big. I clamped it down."

"As I knew you would."

"Handy trick you have there," I said.

"It has been useful a time or two," Ny said in his most flippant, off-handed manner.

"Why'd you never pull it out before?"

Ny stared a moment before softly answering. "Because it affects all humans in the vicinity, and it only ensnares humans."

Okay then. Maybe I should've been happy it at least started to affect me. I had some human banging around in there. Still, I didn't like the idea that I was somehow now immune to a human-specific magic.

I didn't know what flashed across my face, but Ny reached for me, as if to comfort, his hand up to caress. I sidestepped and cleared my throat. "No worries. Let's get this done, okay?" I moved away to inspect the closest sigil on the floor. It looked and tasted like a power draw, which was interesting. They were the marks that allowed them to siphon magic from a source, usually the earth or a magical object of some kind. I was familiar with them because they were tattooed on Harley and Gareth, but these were on the ground. I'd never heard of that. But, then again, what I'd never heard of in regard to magic could fill a whole freaking library.

Looking up and around, I didn't see any sigils other than the large ones painted on the floor. I also didn't feel any major spells lingering. These were what we'd felt outside. Only these and the wards, and maybe something the mages had been doing before Ny hypnotized them. "You sense anything besides these?" I asked Ny. I gestured toward the sigil in front of me before moving a few feet back to look at the room as a whole.

"Nothing," he answered, though he was at a distance now, which made his voice echo in the mostly empty space. It wasn't the scary-sexy Dreamlands internal echo he had, but it still made me tingle. He didn't elaborate because he was crouched, inspecting a different sigil at his feet, one that looked just like the one I'd stared at. In fact, all the sigils painted on the concrete here were the same. They were all power draws.

"Why are these on the ground?" I asked.

Ny took a moment to think, his eyebrows arching as something obviously hit him, but before we could talk about it, a loud crack of thunder pounded through the room. Lightning flashed, and Ny was at my side before we saw who we knew we'd see.

Zeus started yelling, "What do you two imbeciles—" but he stopped as soon as he took in the scene around him.

Ny didn't give much of a chance to take it in. He hit him with shadow, engulfing the Other God so he couldn't move.

"Run," he commanded in his most imperious Outer God voice.

"Not fucking likely," I said, stepping back with my right foot to brace myself as I popped my spear into my hand.

The shadows around Zeus shattered, glass-like shards tinkling to the ground and seeping into the concrete as if they'd never existed. He immediately zipped forward, and Ny's arm shoved me back. I had been braced, but definitely not enough for an Outer God's strength. I went flying and hit my butt a good three feet from where I'd stood.

The moment it had taken Ny to protect me was enough of a window for Zeus, who had him by the throat, both of them wrapped together in crackling electricity. Ny and Zeus were chest to chest, surrounded by a blue-white light. There was no Zeus crack of thunder or streak of lightning. No spark of transference like back on Kadath. Zeus stepped out of the light before it slowly faded from view, almost seeping into Ny's skin, glossing over it like a fine frost. It even tasted like cold winter wind on my tongue. Ny was frozen, stiff and in his original position, stretched into the air. Unmoving.

I screamed but had no time to react in an effective way. It'd lasted mere seconds, and I'd landed a few inches from the power draw sigil I'd been studying—too far to intervene. Scrambling to do something, I shot up but stumbled a step back, landing just inside the lines of the sigil, which pulsed once before a wave of power dived into me. A garbled scream came from my throat as it circled my power and pulled it out and away, shadows leaking from my body like some magical detox, until the power suck was stopped like a dam. I could still feel rolling and amassing, crashing against the stoppage, ready to burst and overtake as soon as it was let loose. The sensation hadn't lasted long, maybe seconds, but it was more than enough to let me know it'd drain my body like a battery.

Zeus, dressed in that same suit, looking like any ridiculous finance bro my ex hung out with, walked around the now-frozen Ny and moved toward his mages, completely ignoring my sounds of struggle as I flailed in the air, trying to get down from the sigil trap. I wasn't being sucked dry anymore, but invisible bonds held me so I could only move my arms and legs a few inches. My mind reeled and I searched for a way out. My magic felt weak, the thrum faint. It was still there, beating, getting a tiny bit louder and stronger with each thump, but it'd take minutes to come back fully, and I wasn't sure I had minutes.

I turned my attention back to the threat. Getting my magic back and loose of this sigil didn't mean shit if the god was about to take me out. I didn't need to worry too much right then, however, because he was solely focused on his henchmen. The mages were somehow still under Ny's spell, swaying slightly with weird, peaceful smiles plastered across their faces. Zeus circled a few times. "I take it you followed them here after they confronted you at your little shop?" he asked, finally looking up at me.

I didn't answer. It was pretty damn obvious at this stage.

He tsk-tsked and squared up in front of the men. "They were to relay a simple message, but I fear they did not do as instructed."

I tested my mouth, my throat, and found I could speak, so I yelled out a breathy, "Let me go!"

He ignored my words and looked over his shoulder at me as he pointed at the injured one. "This one is not at all fond of you for some reason. The other would do as I say, but he overstepped; I'm sure of it. Hence the blood and gore." Zeus tipped the corner of his mouth in a hard line, like a father disappointed in an unruly child, and gave a beleaguered sigh. "It is so very hard to find good human help in this day and age. Soon enough I will be able to use this flute trick as well, but until then, what is it you humans are fond of saying now? If you want something done right…"

He shot out a hand and fried the mages. Literally fried them with lightning in front of my eyes, and he took a solid two minutes to make sure they were properly withered and burnt. Gods, the smell was awful. Disturbingly, the peaceful smiles stayed on their faces the whole time, as if Ny's music rang inside them until the very end. If it did, I hope it gave them some comfort. They were dicks, but no one deserved a painful, burning death via electrocution.

He turned toward me and slowly walked up, studying my flailing, floating body with the same look he'd given the mages. "I'd hoped to be further along before I got you here, Miranda. More's the pity. However, since you and Ny are already here, I will not waste this opportunity."

"What're you doing here?" I asked as I outwardly struggled and internally screamed down my line at DD. The link with DD felt stretched, at a distance, barely there. I hoped it wasn't a massive amount of distance and backup would be here real soon. Soon enough to save me, and if not me, at least save Ny from whatever these sigils were about to do to me.

Zeus laughed at my demanding question. "What is this, one of your human films, where the one you call a villain lays out all their plans so the one you call a hero can thwart them? I think not. You have no need for answers because you will be in no position to care about any of this."

"Villains do villain shit, my guy. Why not live up to the hype?" I was bolder now, not because I wasn't terrified, but because my thrum of magic was pulsing harder, the shadows inside me recovering and pushing their way slowly but surely toward my spear with every single beat of my heart. I didn't know what would happen when those inner shadows reached my clenched fist, but I knew it had umph behind it whatever it was—hopefully enough umph to get me free and not dead.

"I am not your villain, Miranda, although it may be easier for your human mind to think of me as such. I am your savior."

"It's Randy, asshole, and I'm sick of telling you. Also, I think you have your godly roles confused. Saviors are all about sacrifice. I don't see you sacrificing shit."

"I am prepared to sacrifice you and everyone else who stands in my path to save the human realm from itself. Your kind is weak, requires a firm guiding hand. I am the god who will provide it for you."

Ridiculous logic, but I didn't have time to argue about it more because the front windows blew out, and I tasted Gareth's and Harley's magic on my tongue a second before wrenching, sucking pain hit my body and stopped my magic in its tracks.

# Fifteen

A whole lot of shit happened I couldn't keep track of. Mostly because of the pain. Whatever Zeus had done to dam up the effects of the sigil broke open, and the power washed over me full force. All I felt was painful draining. Weak shadows leaked from my body as I struggled to rein them in, but I was stuck fast, unable to do anything but feel the pain of the magic inside me, the magic I knew was connected to who I was, as well as my life force—or whatever you might want to call it—slipping out.

I saw the flair of the sigil, a flash of grayish-purple pulsing in time with every suck and pull of my magic. Then, a clawed hand ripped across the painted form of the sigil and scraped a deep gouge in the concrete, breaking up the painted sigil and, apparently, its power.

I crumpled to the floor, gasping from the residual pain of the spell and the pain of hitting the ground hard. Rich was there beside me, a hand marked with claws extended to help. "Randy? Are you okay?"

I didn't have time to answer, because as soon as I caught my breath and my brain and magic both realized I was freed, I steeled myself for a blow, ready to fight off Zeus. He was a little busy, however, dodging magical blows from Harley as Gareth shielded her.

"Protect Ny!" I shouted at Rich, and he went over and crouched in a defensive position close to his friend. Ny was his friend, which was likely why he actually did what I kind of rudely demanded he do, but I had no time for niceties.

For one, my magic was thrumming like mad, building up again almost twofold as if it was a living, conscious thing, angry someone had dared try to take it in the first place. For another, DD was zipping around me, frantic, trying to get my attention. I calmed it as best I could down the line as I gave it another command. "Shore up Gareth's ward," I gritted out as I pulled myself up to my knees, digging my spear into the ground to then raise myself to standing, a little wobbly but gaining back strength and magic with each passing second.

DD did as I asked, creating an effective shield between Harley and Gareth and an increasingly pissed-off Zeus. They couldn't have been fighting for more than a minute, but I think for a god like him, he'd view it as about fifty-five seconds too long when dealing with humans, even if they were powerful mages like Harley and Gareth.

"Enough!" he roared, his voice a cracking boom filling the nearly empty space. He zapped DD with lightning, which jumped from the DD shield and branched out in an arc of electricity to sizzle the wards around Harley and Gareth, kind of like we were inside one of those lightning ball things with electricity in vivid shades of white and blue arching and crackling all around. My big guy was powerful, even more so now he could hold a bigger charge of magic from me and Ny. Harley was likely the greatest mage of our time. I'd seen her power do amazing things, even rip apart inter-dimensionally built churches. Still, they were mages. Humans. Not made to fight a god. Gareth's wards cracked and he went flying, taking only a hint of the power Zeus threw at him, but enough to knock him out of the fight momentarily. Harley grunted in pain but kept up her assault, firing green globes of magic at Zeus. Wherever they hit, they sizzled and scorched his suit and skin, but both healed immediately. It looked like more of an annoyance than anything else.

He twisted his hand, and I smelled his intent before the next bolt came. DD dodged it effectively, but Harley was right in the crossfire. Luckily, I reached her first. Or my spear did. I'd stretched it out as I ran toward her, willing it forward, trying to intercept the lightning before it could strike.

My spear caught the bolt and absorbed the blow, but it still stung. Like really stung. The electricity raced down the spear, flying into my hand, through my arm, and up my shoulder, causing pain to shoot through me before leaving a tingling numbness behind. I screamed. I couldn't help it. It did not feel good.

Gareth struggled to get back up, and Harley moved toward me. No time for niceties, I barked at her, "You and Gareth stay the fuck back," as I turned my full attention to Zeus.

DD was already bubbled around me, but it was shaky and worn from the blows it had taken. My spear arm also felt shaky, unusable, but my internal shadows, now fully gathered, once again headed to it. They reversed the path of the lightning, traveling from shoulder to arm to hand and melding with the spear, giving me magical strength.

Zeus's eyes widened a touch, but his lips curled back with disdain. There was no banter. No time for it. I was too busy lashing out with my spear, which flung shadow from its end, sailing it like the line of a whip right toward Zeus's stupid face. The blow struck true, and a small gash welled across his cheek. It didn't heal right away like Harley's blows, and I noticed with more than a little cold satisfaction that his hand shook slightly when he reached up to wipe the small drops of welling blood away.

He sent another bolt, which I sidestepped with a smooth shadow walk, coming back several steps closer to him. But it was too late. He'd already gathered clouds, lightning, and thunder to him, cocooning himself. Creating the same magic he'd used to get here in order to take him away. Pure hate flashed on his face, directed at me, as he vanished.

"Son of a *bitch*!" I screamed at no one as I clutched my spear even tighter. It seemed he was only brave enough to come at me when he had an advantage. As soon as I landed any type of blow, he bounced. Such a cowardly asshole.

I looked around me to check the damage. Harley was helping Gareth to his feet, but both looked physically fine. Rich lingered by Ny, no longer crouched in defense but looking worried still. Probably because Ny was frozen in place, unmoving, as he'd been since Zeus did whatever the hell he did to him.

I scurried over and popped my spear back out of the human realm. Zeus was gone, the mages were discarded toast, and I steered clear of any of the sucking sigils on the ground. Call it a very clear lesson learned with those things.

Ny stood rigid, slightly stretched, his head tilted up and neck long, just as it had been when Zeus had him by the throat. His whole body was taut, every muscle frozen in strain, his dusty brown skin tight and his usually luscious lips pulled back in a grimace.

"What is this?" I asked Rich.

"Because Zeus has some of Ny's power from the Book of Knowing, and because he's been in Ny's human skin before, I think he has some sort of control over it. This human form of Ny."

Harley and Gareth had walked up by then, each studying Ny's body. Harley was the most knowledgeable person I knew, so I turned to her next. "How do we fix this? Unstick him or unfreeze him or whatever."

She moved out from under Gareth's shoulder. He slumped some before he took on his own weight, and I reached to steady him as I looked at Harley for answers. She circled Ny, touched the air around him as certain sigils on her arms glowed, and stopped to stare hard into his upturned face. She looked at me, and the sadness in her eyes told me before she even said anything. "I have no idea, Randy. And don't know who would. This is Dreamlands magic, Outer and Other God magic, which is way over my head."

"Shit, shit, shit," I muttered, shaking from the adrenaline come-down mixed with very serious worry about the Prince. I forced myself to think through, try to reason with what happened before in the Dreamlands. There, though, Zeus had taken over his human body. He was made of shadows, like me, so I was working through some way I could try to push shadow through him to clear out whatever icy power was making him frozen, when Rich handed me a phone.

The sudden appearance of a phone in my face was jarring, but I heard the tinny voice of Mia on the thing, so I snatched it from him and put it on speaker so we all could hear.

"Mia?" I asked.

"Randy. Listen. If Ny is stuck, like frozen or something, right? He needs part of the Dreamlands to help. Or part of himself. Something Outer God-ish. His human form, as it is and without his usual access to the Book of Knowing, can get locked down with power similar to his, which Zeus has. Only another similar power can unstick it."

"My power won't work?" I asked. What she said followed the same line of thought I'd had, but not exactly.

"Not now. Or I don't think so. Not without you getting a lot more knowledgeable on how to use it or access it all real quick. And the longer he's stuck..."

Mia hesitated, so I bit out, "Tell me."

"The longer he's stuck, the more likely it is he'll always be stuck, his human form creating a prison for his Outer God self."

Gareth let out an uncharacteristic "fuck" as my eyes pricked with tears. No more Ny? I couldn't have that.

"You know this from the book?"

A softer "yes" was followed by more explanation. "Rich and I've been working on it. I have more access and knowledge, especially if it happens to coincide with things, people, or places I know."

I took a long breath, feeling the weight of my necklace as my mind whirled. "We need some type of power from either the Dreamlands or an Outer God?"

"Not smart, Randy," Harley said beside me, apparently already working out the course of action like I was, even as Mia firmly said yes for all of us to hear.

"Thanks, sis. Love you," I called before hanging up on her. I didn't have time to waste, and she'd given me the info I needed. I had to step up and do the damn thing.

"Randy, think this through," Harley said, her dark eyes boring into mine.

"You may not think so, Harley, but I did. I have to do it. For Ny."

"Do what?" Rich asked, still a little behind.

"Go get whatever it is Ny needs," I calmly answered.

"Seriously, girl? You don't even know what it is he needs to help him, much less where to go or even how to get there on your own."

"I know where to go to get all the answers and supplies I need. Last time Zeus used Ny's own powers against him, the Writhing helped. I've been to where it likes to hang. Plus, I already have a direct link right here." I whipped the silver key over my head, clutching it in my hand as I let out a long breath. "Step back."

"Wait," I heard Gareth say, but I had no time to waste. If what Mia said was true, the longer Ny was frozen, the harder it'd be to thaw him. I needed Ny, for lots of reasons, so I'd do whatever it took to get him back. This wasn't stepping without looking, despite what Harley thought. Not exactly. I'd walked this path before, for a similar reason, so it was logical to do it again.

Darker, heavier shadows circled my body, called into being by the shadows of magic in my body. They worked their way up, encasing my legs and waist in a blink. They were a little slower going from there, so I had time to say, "Don't worry, big guy. Be right back," before they encased my head. There was cause to worry a little. The shadows weren't the Writhing from the Dreamlands, so I wasn't 100 percent certain they'd be able to reach where I needed to go. Then, if I did get there, I wasn't sure a certain robed, skeletal door guard would help me out. Lots of questions, lots of uncertainty, but sometimes the only way out was through, even if the way through was all shadows and darkness.

# Sixteen

I was back in those damn robes. Not that I had a big issue with the black, flowing robes in theory. They were kind of cute and definitely comfy, but they weren't my choice, and that was the rub. Why I didn't show up in the dream cave in my everyday clothes was a mystery I wasn't too keen on exploring right then. There was a more pressing need, namely getting some Writhing to come with me back to the human realm or getting the guard to help somehow. Either worked for me as long as they worked for Ny.

I'd returned to the point where the slick black stone walls and floor of the cave sloped down, so the first place I checked was the walls. Where the Writhing had hung about before was only black stone space. No shadow in sight. Or, at least, no churning, solid, power-ful-ass shadows, so I made my way down toward the well, which was usually filled with the things.

As the floor leveled, I felt a pull from my magic, an internal thrum somehow telling me without words I was on the right track. I picked up the pace and burst into Umar at-Tawil's space maybe a little too quick and slightly breathless. The guard of the silver gate stood still as death, which was fitting as the whole black-robe-and-faceless-presence thing they had going on reminded me of a Halloween grim reaper, only much scarier. They seemed not at all surprised to see me. Actually didn't think much would faze them, being an eternal servant to an Outer God and all.

"Randy Carter," they said, their tone expectant, as if they had been waiting for me. Which, given the fact they left me with the key, maybe they had been waiting since the last time I was here.

"What's up?" I replied, which was idiotic, but the etiquette of interdimensional beings was not something I'd learned yet. I was too busy sprinting for the well to concern myself with it too much. I looked into blackness and saw only darkness and empty stone. There wasn't a damn speck of Writhing there.

"Where is it?" I asked. It was probably more of a demand, but I needed those stronger shadows, and I still had no idea how to get it into the human realm even when I found it, so I didn't exactly have time for hide-and-seek.

"It is not for me to say," they replied.

"Okay. Look. I don't have time for this mess. I need straight answers. Do you know what is happening with Ny in the human realm?"

"I am no Outer God. I do not possess omnipotence or the ability to freely see from realm to realm," they answered. I could've sworn there was a slight hint of annoyance in their voice, but it was hard to say because it had the weird, eternal quality all the really old beings could take on. Still, annoyed or not, I had to press them.

"Well, let me tell you. Ny's frozen, and apparently he needs something from either the Dreamlands or wherever it is the Outer Gods come from to help unfreeze him. I figure the Writhing will work since it helped last time something similar went down. So, again, I ask, where is it?"

"Again, I must reply, it is not for me to say."

I yelled. A full-on scream of rage and annoyance and hurt and uncertainty, my head tilted toward the ceiling and my fists clenched at my sides. The cave shook with my sound and my magic hummed under my skin. I was sick of not knowing, of not being able to do something, and of always being several steps behind everyone else in this rigged game.

"Randy Carter," Umar at-Tawil called. I turned hard eyes their way, and they continued. "You ask questions I cannot answer. Ask another."

"Is there anything here I could take back with me to the human realm to help Ny?"

"No." It was a firm answer, and they gave me no more. Verbally. They did shuffle their feet a half step so they were no longer fully centered in the old frame of the door they guarded. The odd, almost fidgeting movement brought my eyes right to the door, and the tiny silver lock smack in the middle of it. Tricksy guard. They couldn't say for whatever reason, but they were trying to help as best they could.

"Will I find something to help Ny if I go through the door there?" I asked, pointing behind them.

"Perhaps. I cannot say for certain, as I do not know. I know there is nothing here for you. Your choice is to enter the door or return with nothing."

I let out a shaky breath. Knowing the door led to the home of the Outer Gods wasn't exactly comforting, but I needed to help Ny. It was literally the only choice, really.

"I can open it with my key, right?" I wanted to double-check I was on the right path.

"Yes. The silver key opens the door to the land of the Outer Gods. As you have the key still, you may open the door and enter. What may happen to you after, however, I do not know and cannot guess."

"Have you been in there?" I asked, my nerves getting the best of me for a moment.

"I was created there, so yes. Have witnessed others come and go over the course of my service."

"Okay," I whispered before I blinked hard and said it again more firmly. More surely. "Okay. I want to enter, please."

"You have the key. All you need do is use it." They shuffled more to the side, giving me plenty of space to get at the door.

I couldn't waver or hesitate. I didn't know what would happen in there, but I knew without me going, Ny would be stuck frozen in his human body. I couldn't have that, so I squared my shoulders and moved to do the damn thing.

"Any advice?" I asked the guard, though I didn't look at them. They turned their hooded head my way and I knew, if I wanted, I could look, see what they were underneath, but I was already doing one scary thing. Didn't need to see Umar at-Tawil's true form while I was at it.

"Listen, watch, take in everything. Also, try to land softly."

Once again, vague as hell, but what else could I have expected? My hand trembled as I raised the silver key waist height to insert it in the glinting silver lock. Turning it, I heard a click and felt the door move inward slightly. I pushed and felt more give, until the door freely swung open onto nothingness, and I was sucked into another unknown.

IT WAS SPACE. LIKE honest-to-gods deep space, so I didn't really understand how I was breathing, much less how my screams were echoing in my ears and not just inside my head. Wasn't space supposed to be a vacuum or something? After long seconds of feeling like I was falling while also being weightless, a very odd sensation, I stopped the screaming. I wasn't hurting or anything, so I needed to be more thoughtful. Figured there was little I could do but fall to whatever I was falling toward, so I tried to brace myself.

The impact came a minute later when I landed in a belly flop on a fluffy maroon velvet couch. I lay there, my eyes open and my nose pressed to the fabric, trying to inventory my body. I had my usual weight back, which was comforting. I was stationary. I was unhurt, the couch having cushioned the blow of my freefall. But who knew where I was or what was lurking about, so once I figured out I was good, I did a half pushup to survey the room.

It was lush as hell. Velvet, silk, and satin everywhere. Everything from the furniture to the walls to the floor was draped in jewel tones. Actual jewels glinted throughout too, woven into fabrics and embedded in precious metals. The sconces on the wall dripped with fat, smoking candles, which added the perfect mood lighting to the space. Right in the middle of the room, sitting crossed-leg and grinning with his ridiculous, slightly wonky, all-too-average grin, was Azathoth, the Blind King, Ny's very own sire, the one who'd pulled things from chaos into being. The closest thing to a leader of all the gods, Outer and Other, I knew of in any realm, sat there all chill, radiating waves of awesome, terrifying power. He was the same dude who seemed to like me for whatever reason, and had once—in the middle of an Other Gods ball—given me the same mundane, lopsided grin he was currently giving me as I struggled to get up from his couch. No big deal. Not at all.

# SEVENTEEN

"Welcome, Randy. I'm so glad you can join me in my home." He looked like he had at the ball, a regular white dude I'd run into on the streets of Columbus. His sandy-brown hair was trimmed neat, and his skin was smooth but unextraordinary. He even had slight laugh lines and crow's feet, almost like he was an average forty-year-old guy. He wasn't, and I was again reminded of this as the power in his voice washed over my senses, his magic jolting me, tasting like dust and time and unfathomable old things.

I wasn't exactly glad to see him. He was the head honcho of everything apparently, and of all I knew about gods, it seemed the more power they had, the more unpredictable they were. With the exception of Ny. Still, I wasn't about to be rude to a king in his own home, my Midwestern manners running deep, so I said, "Thanks for having me."

"So polite and kind, Randy Carter. So unlike all I see day in and day out in the places I inhabit."

I studied the Outer God, the one some called the Blind Idiot King. He didn't look blind or idiotic. He had an odd light in his eyes, but it could simply be the power he had, which was a hell of a lot. I suspected he was even tamping it down some right then. He was all knowing, all powerful, all everything in the chaos of creation. I couldn't really understand fully what it meant, so I needed to brush the existential questions aside and focus on why I was there. Not before I tucked the silver key away again, stuffing it in my pants pocket as discreetly as possible, like I wasn't trying to hide something the dude had to already know I had on me.

He watched, a half-amused smile on his face as I pushed myself up to sit. Once I was upright and had some sense of balance, I said, "Ny is in trouble."

A sigh rumbled through the room, snaking across my skin and the walls, causing both to quiver. "My children are often in trouble, of one form or another. It is enough to drive a father mad, you know?"

I nodded like I knew, but I didn't have kids, much less Outer God kids, so I had no real idea.

Azathoth continued, rising smoothly from the floor as he said, "However, I have less problems with Nyarlathotep. Have had, since he discovered you and your future together in the Book of Knowing so long ago. It gave him drive and purpose beyond himself. I do wish Yog and Nog had the same."

He sat on the couch next to me, his arm brushing against mine, causing my magic to flair and shrink back as if afraid. Even the robe shifted as if wanting to give him plenty of space. Despite the magical reaction, I didn't personally sense danger from him, so I pressed my case. "I need some Writhing, or maybe something else? I don't know. All I know is Ny is trapped in his human form somehow, and I need a piece of the Dreamlands or your home to help set him free."

He blinked his eyes at me, and I saw the swirl of darkness there for the first time. Unlike Ny's ever-present and large night-sky eyes, Azathoth's darkness was contained to a small section of his iris, which flowed and changed, flashing various colors of creation, moving from sky to land to sea to things I had no idea about. It was a little nauseating, to be honest, but I pushed down the feeling of unmooring it gave me. After long beats, he asked me, "You wish him free, despite who he is?"

"What's that supposed to mean?" I asked, maybe being a little too defensive with the King of the Outer Gods, but whatever. Ny was Ny, and I needed him. I wanted him, as he was and definitely unstuck.

"Nyarlathotep has lived eons, Randy. Done unimaginable things. Was once very like his siblings in his actions and drives."

"Not anymore. You said so yourself."

Azathoth wrinkled his brow and studied my face before he responded. "I understand." Softly, with true sadness echoing in his godly voice, he said, "I miss who you were, but that is not who you are. As Ny is no longer who he was."

I really needed to get something for Ny and hightail it back to the human realm pronto, but his last statement opened a whole can of worms for me. He'd known Hecate, had a relationship with her, according to Ny. Likely even made her. What he'd said indicated he even missed her in a way that made my heart ache a little for him. Because he was who he was, because he had once deeply cared for Hecate, I had so many questions for him—questions only he could answer—so I had to take a little bit of my time to try to get a few important answers. Those answers would help Ny too, in a different way. Help all of us back in Columbus.

I swallowed hard and pushed through the uncertainty to ask the really important, and really indelicate, thing. "How did Zeus kill her?"

I didn't need to explain to him who "her" was. His eyes flashed dark and cold before he reached out and patted my hand in a paternal way. "She was drained. Then killed. It's the only way."

I jolted at the basic answer to the looming question we'd had for a while: How do you kill a god? Apparently you drain them. Zeus had the knowledge to do it. "He drained her of magic, so, what? She became killable?"

"She became something closer to human, something his magic could erase."

"Her magic wasn't entirely erased," I said, looking down at my robe-clad form, thinking about my spear and torch and DD and the thurm of magic humming in my gut even then.

"No. He did not have enough knowledge of sigils back then, as it was more Hecate's specialty. He had yet to study for centuries, learn how to harness crafted magic to take the once drained. Make all the energy his."

"Magic, and energy, doesn't die. Only changes," I said, a line I'd used so often lately in my magical learning.

He smiled and gave my shoulder a playful tap with his. "Yes. It changes. In this case, inhabiting the growing form of a human in its mother's womb many, many centuries later."

"Why me though? Why this human?"

"Because it always was you."

Tears formed at the corners of my eyes, but I couldn't stop them. I needed this answer, so let the tears fall. "What if it chose wrong? I'm no one special. I don't come from money, don't have any genius, don't have extraordinary talent in any other thing. I've failed and hurt so many people. I'm just Randy, a regular person, not some god with all the answers."

"Do you believe the gods you've met have all the answers?"

I really thought about it for a minute. How Hecate and Ny and all the Other Gods were obviously fooled in serious ways. Azathoth had even lost someone he cared for, by tough choice or being too slow or unaware. Zeus was causing havoc, but he definitely didn't know everything... had failed a time or two. They might have all the power, a fount of magic inside, but they didn't know everything. Or, if they did know everything, they still were prone to make stupid choices like any human. Like me.

Something clicked in my head then. I didn't need to know everything—couldn't know everything. I could go on despite it, maybe even because of it. Godly or no, I had power and a will to use it to help others, the people I loved, and general humans to boot. I would fight when I needed to fight, think through stuff, get a helping hand from time to time, and fall and get back up and try again. Trying was the key, and I could do that all day, every day. Striving was a very human trait after all.

"Gotcha," I said, firm and true.

King Azathoth stared deep into my eyes, but I didn't flinch. I wasn't afraid of what was there, even if I should've been.

He smiled big and wide and cackled out a laugh. "Oh, I do believe you now do, Randy. I do believe you do." The king jumped from his place and hurried to a brass tea cart against the opposite wall. As he looked through covered dishes there, searching for something, he called back to me, "Zeus was unable to contain and transfer Hecate's magic before."

It was an abrupt change of subject, so it took me a minute to catch up. I'd had a major mental shift, after all. Eventually I asked, "Now?" hoping he'd fill in the blank I left dangling.

"He learned to use sigils and spells. He can not only drain, but siphon. Not like your human mages, who temporarily hold power, but make it a part of his own internal magical source."

"Shit," I muttered, worrying my lip. This was not a great turn of events, but I already knew Zeus needed to be stopped, so the new info did little to change the game plan.

He muttered something to himself before his voice raised in an odd question. "Do you not have mages at your side?"

Hell yeah, I did. One of the best around, in fact. Plus, Gareth was no slouch in the mage department. They could work a sigil, no problem. They also had access to ones Zeus created. Harley might not be able to spellcraft naturally, but she'd study the hell out of the sigils in the abandoned building and take them apart with her intention and her knowledge. Make them useful for us.

"Okay. Got it. Thanks for the heads-up. I really need help with the Ny situation first."

He let out a tiny noise of triumph and scooped up a Persian-blue container that fit perfectly in his palm. "I knew I stored it somewhere," he said to himself before striding back across the room and handing the container to me like a prize.

It weighed next to nothing in my palm and was less than extra-ordinary in any outward way. I moved to peek under the lid, but Azathoth stilled my hand. "No," he said. "Do not release it here. It is Writhing, which will push out any other magic trapping our dear Prince. However, it is tricky to transport and keep in one place. I coaxed it in here, but once freed, it can only be controlled for a brief period of time. It still holds too much primordial chaos, always driven to go back to its point of origin. Do not release it until you are with Ny and can direct its actions immediately for your purpose."

I narrowed my eyes at him. "Is this the Writhing from the cave?"

He met my question with a wonky grin. "I wished you to visit me here."

"Which was why Umar at-Tawil was all cryptic and shit," I mut-tered. Of course they wouldn't narc on their king. "Next time, maybe just send an invite."

"I shall," he replied, giving me a slight bow as he did. "Now, you must hurry. You're not too late, but you may soon be." Leading me to a door hidden behind an intricately woven tapestry of a desert oasis, he said, "You may return to your original spot in the human realm from here. Do not open any doors in the hallway behind this entrance. Do not deviate from the path. At the end of the hallway, you will find shadow, and all you need do is walk through it with intention."

I nodded in understanding and rushed to open the door. Before I stepped through, I asked, "Why do you interfere in some things but not others? Obviously you took the Writhing from the cave, knowing I'd need it and would come. Couldn't you have saved Hecate and prevented all this shit from happening?" I wasn't angry when I asked. Couldn't be. If he'd done what I thought he might have the power to do, I wouldn't be who and where I was.

Azathoth froze in place, as if this obvious question was totally unexpected. "Would you wish it so?"

I thought about it but kind of already knew the answer. Without all the mess, I wouldn't have Ny and Gareth. There'd be no Harley in my life or Merry's. Mia might be better, but she'd not be the same. Too much hinged on the details for me to wish them away. "No."

He smiled. "Then why does it matter?"

I snorted. It was a cop-out if I ever heard one, but what should I have expected? The creator of Outer and Other Gods, the realms I knew and many I didn't, wasn't required to answer questions about why he did the stuff he did. He simply did. I realized some part of me was happy about it. I didn't really want all the answers, Where would be the fun in that?

Also, oddly enough, I thought Azathoth might have grown on me. Before I left, I threw out one last question. "Will we have another meeting like this one day?"

He winked and asked back, "Why would I spoil the surprise?" before laughing and saying, "Go help our Prince, Randy Carter, in all the ways you can."

I knew I wasn't getting any more out of him, and to be honest, I'd gotten a shit-ton of info and reassurance somehow along with the help I came for, so I wasn't going to push.

# Eighteen

Azathoth was in my theoretical rearview when the large door clicked shut, and I hurried down the hall. I had no reason to look back and every reason to hurry the hell up. I tried not to look at the doors I passed, but I did take in some of the hallway. It was dark, of course, like everything else that involved the Outer Gods in one way or another. The proportions felt odd, as if the doors I perceived as only being one or two feet off to either side were actually much farther away. They loomed large—dark, cavernous things with ornate frames, each slightly different from the others even with the little I saw of each one. Some had shifts in color, some jutted out more into the hallway. There were a few doors where sound pushed through, and I heard slithering and scraping, noises of attempted escapes of things large and likely horrifying I definitely would not investigate even on a good day. All of it tasted like a jumble of magic and time and space I couldn't immediately untangle and didn't really want to. It was a weird and creepy-as-hell place I was happy to scurry down as quickly as possible.

I was startled when I caught a flash of a hand reaching out of a door frame ahead of me. I side-stepped out of the way, but I didn't feel like who or whatever was coming through the door was actually reaching for me. When they stepped through, they stopped, as if startled by my presence. Whatever could roam around freely in the hallway was not something I wanted to interact with, so I froze. The person was tall and thin, like Slender-Man levels of both. Could've been an odd trick of the proportions and space of the hallway again, but they wore the suit and tie like in those creepy photoshopped images of the hoax online. Their face was also fuzzy. Not the blank and swirling nothingness of a night gaunt, but as if it were an intentional feature to make them more unknowable.

The dude took a step back, leaning in the doorframe to study me from head to toe, and even though I couldn't quite see it, I had the impression a smile spread across his thin and hazy lips. He folded his long arms across his chest and inclined his head toward his other side, silently urging me to continue down the hallway. Right past him. I took the chance to glance back a second toward the door I'd entered from, where Azathoth may have been still hanging out. The King may have been a lot, but he was a known entity in some ways, one I sensed wouldn't hurt me if he could help it. This dude, however, tasted of wet wood and slimy field greens left sitting in the fridge a touch too long, a magic I wasn't familiar with and didn't want to get to know. His power pulsed out in bursts, filling the hallway. Not exactly like King Azathoth yet still too much for my liking.

Stuck between where I'd been and where I needed to be, I didn't know how to proceed. If I needed to fight, I had the Writhing in one hand, but I needed to let it loose on Ny, not here. The only other thing I thought could help, and might work in this place, was my spear. Didn't know if I could or should bust it out, but I did. I thought about it, and it popped right into my hand, all solid shadow metal and sharp god-cutting tip, which was a relief. I had to get to Ny, didn't know what type of shit this new entity might try to pull, and I didn't have time to plan uncertain, posturing games with the guy.

As soon as he saw the spear, he straightened from his lean, his arms unfolding and dangling to his side. His head slowly tilted left, then right, and I felt his eyes roaming over me again, more slowly this time. Assessing. A whisper of a word echoed in the few feet between us, making the hairs on my arm stand on end. "Miranda," the guy said, though how I knew he said it was unclear because it didn't look like his hazy mouth moved.

Annoyed with the fact that everyone creepy and potentially evil in these places refused to use my preferred name, I tightened my body and let my sarcasm fly. I was so done with this bullshit and had places to be. "Randy, and I'm just going to scooch by you, okay?"

I stepped, he tensed, and I was more than ready to throw something his way quickly, then run as fast as I could to the end of this weird-ass hallway. Didn't need to fight to the death with some unknown when Ny was in trouble, and I wanted to stay breathing in general, so a hit-and-run situation would be my best bet. Then I tasted Azathoth's unique brand of power on my tongue. A deep rumble tore through the space, leaving everything, including me, a little shaky. Whoever the dude was relaxed his stance, took two big-ass steps back, and centered themselves in the open doorway, a good few feet away from me.

I didn't waste time. I ran as quickly as I could with a big spear in one hand and the tiny blue pot in my other, feeling the dude's gaze follow me as I passed him. No time to think too hard on whatever the hell type of weird confrontation I'd almost had. Ny needed help, so I needed to get to the shadows Azathoth told me would be somewhere ahead of me.

I didn't stop running until I saw familiar shadows pressing in on me and tasted a darkness I knew well. My spear wasn't needed anymore, so I popped it back to wherever it went, giving a bit of thanks. What-ever magic allowed me to access the weapon worked there when DD couldn't for some reason. I shook off the fear and adrenaline of the last several minutes and stepped into the chilly and comforting embrace of shadows, feeling the rush of becoming one with them as I clung to my little bowl of Writhing and set all my intention toward home and what it held for me.

Azathoth had told me I'd shadow walk back to where I'd come from, but it wasn't exactly the same. For me, shadow walking was more like jumping from point to point in a fluid flash. Here then there then another spot. It happened quickly, but it had definite points of contact along the way, spots marking a sense of distance. When I stepped into the shadows of the hallway and became one with them, almost instantaneously my feet felt solid again, anchored in the human world to dingy concrete in the old, abandoned business where we'd just fought with Zeus. It was like teleportation instead of movement, a slight yet not insignificant difference, but one I couldn't think about at the moment. The new Nightcrawler experience would have to wait until I somehow used the bowl of Writhing I was white knuckling in my hand.

DD saw or sensed me first, its frantic shaking traveling up and around my body, circling to ensure I was whole and well. I sent calming coos down our mental line but couldn't waste a lot of time with chitchat. Harley saw me next and said nothing, but her long, lean body visibly loosened some.

I couldn't take in much of anything else as I rushed over to everyone gathered around the still-stuck Ny and asked, "How long was I gone?" It wasn't info I needed or could do anything about, but it felt important to know.

"Maybe twenty seconds," Gareth said. His voice sounded heavy, and his eyes trailed over me, looking from head to toe as his shoulders shifted from high and tight to their more normal broad and relaxed position. Only slightly relaxed though, because he turned back toward Ny, concern etched deep in his face.

"You get what we need?" Rich asked, stepping aside to let me stand in front of Ny.

"Yep, though what it'll do and how exactly it'll do it is up in the air." I twisted the lid off the bright-blue metal bowl. I saw a glimpse of tight darkness, thick and impenetrable, inside the bowl before it burst out, pushing Rich, Harley, Gareth and DD back several feet so it surrounded only me and Ny. Inside the thick bubble of churning and thinking dark, I was lost for action or knowledge or plans, so I went with what always seemed to work with magical things. All my intention and love and need filled the words as I said, "Free him."

The Writhing slithered around, moving up and over Ny, reaching into his body through his nostrils and his ears and his wide-open eyes. Slowly, it seeped in, and as more of it disappeared from around us, flowing into him, his body began to shake. Ny trembled, then jerked. His hands clenched and he blinked his eyes rapidly. Then he crumpled to the floor just like I had earlier, smacking hard against the concrete.

"We really need something to cushion our falls," I muttered, my fear and stress seeping away from me in the same way the Writhing was now leaking from a coughing Ny, pouring out of his mouth to gather and churn at our feet.

I bent to rest a hand on his back and rub circles there. "Ny? You okay in there?"

He held up a finger as he continued to cough, getting all those thick and thinking shadows out of his system before turning to me with grateful eyes. "Yes, thanks to you, my sweetling." The Writhing arched over us and fell in waves, crashing to the ground so we were no longer secluded in its sphere. Immediately DD jumped in, skimming me quickly for any signs of distress before hovering close to Ny with an anxious shake.

Ny nudged the worried DD with a tilt of his chin and grabbed my hand and raised us both to standing before pulling me into a deep hug. I felt Gareth's arms wrap around us, wordlessly supporting while radiating his usual calm comfort. When we broke apart, Rich reached out to tap his friend on the shoulder and gave him a wolfish grin. "Thought you might be stuck for a while there."

"He would've been if Randy hadn't gone off to wherever she went in the Dreamlands," Harley said. It seemed she was still a little sore about me leaving without more convo. Oh well. I did what I did. Couldn't turn back time. At least I didn't think I had that power, though I know Ny did at one point. I'd thought it through, but when there were few options, even informed choices could seem reckless.

Ny'd been flexing and shifting, testing the control over his human body, but paused at Harley's words. "You traveled to the Dreamlands for the Writhing?"

"Well, not exactly." I hedged because I really didn't want to go into all of it right then.

"Where did you go?" Gareth asked, his tone a little too sharp for my liking. He was my big guy, one of my loves, but he wasn't the boss of me.

"First, I went where I needed to go and did what I had to do to get Ny back." I reached up to push some of Ny's flopping, thick black hair off his forehead so I could stare into his spacey eyes. "I had to get you back."

"I know, love. I would do the same. However, we must discuss where you went and what you did."

I sighed. "I'll tell you, but it's not going to be a big debate. Not now." I said it to Ny but turned to catch everyone in my stare. "Get it? We'll hash it out detail by detail later. I know you all love to do that. Right now, though, I just want to be happy Ny is back in control of himself. Most of all, I want to rest. Maybe take a long bath or something."

"Fine," Harley said with a curt nod. "We'll hold all questions for later."

Everyone muttered their agreement too, so I spilled.

"Okay. Long story short, I went to the cave from my dreams, chatted with Umar at-Tawil, opened the door he guards with my silver key, then ended up in a very Moroccan-inspired study-type area with King Azathoth. He's the one who gave me the bowl of Writhing and sent me on my way."

I got slack-jawed looks all around.

Ny's starry eyes darkened, and a tick fluttered across his sharp jaw. I stared at him, eyes open, hip cocked, and arms crossed on my chest. They'd agreed to let it go for now, and I would hold him to the agreement. We all needed rest, at least for the rest of the day.

Ny reined himself in, as I knew he would. "Very well. We can all discuss this tomorrow."

No one else seemed too happy, but they kept their word and zipped their lips about it.

"What about this?" I asked, gesturing down at the Writhing still churning at our feet.

"It will return to where it belongs on its own if no longer required here," Ny said. "Leave it and let us go home."

"Sounds like a plan," I said, leaning into him. His body felt hard and hot and sizzling with power. Solid and strong in a way I needed to touch to help my brain confirm he was unstuck and back to his usual self. He took my weight without a word, letting me melt into him as he shuffled us along.

"Oh, Harley. See these sigils scattered on the ground? They're extra special, according to Azathoth. Can you take some time to study them soon? They'll probably come in handy with the Zeus stuff later."

Her face was still hard, but she gave a silent acknowledgement before focusing on the sigils in question. She'd have those things figured out in no time.

"You drive?" Gareth asked, coming up to my side.

"Yep."

"Keys," he demanded, and I didn't scoff or push back. He could drive my tiny Mini Cooper if he wanted. Was probably even a good idea. I tossed him my keys and we all exited the building, leaving the Writhing and the burnt mages and the power-sucking sigils behind. I had no more bandwidth to discuss much of anything. Only enough for good-byes and to let my guys lead me to my car.

# Nineteen

Ny held up well on the ride back to German Village, except he stayed mostly rigid and quiet. As soon as we entered his house, he flopped onto his couch, exhaustion carving lines in his usually smooth, golden-brown face. He leaned his head back, covering his eyes with his forearms and going totally still. Not frozen still, but enough to have me twisting my hands in worry. I looked at Gareth, whose eyes were still hard and a smidge angry, more brown than hazel at the moment. He gave a clipped nod toward Ny as he threw my keys on the table.

I wasn't all about this little tantrum he was having when I'd only done what needed to be done, but Ny being in a bit of a state after an ordeal was my main concern at the moment. "Ny?" I asked, moving to sit beside him on the couch and angling my body so I faced him.

He grunted but said nothing.

"You need something?" I asked.

He turned deep-space eyes on me, blinking hard a few times before he leaned in, letting his upper body fall along the back of the couch so he eventually slid into me. "I need to feel you," he muttered, "know you are here, I am here, and we are both whole."

"Of course we are," I said, running my fingers through his thick black hair and down over his crinkled forehead.

A deep sigh came from Gareth, and he put in his two cents. "There is no 'of course' in this, Randy."

I turned hard navy eyes his way and bit out, "I won't apologize for doing what I had to do to bring Ny back to us."

"It was dangerous," Gareth said.

"Reckless," Ny said.

"Ultimately, completely fine and exactly what we needed." I didn't want to fight with them after the day we'd had, but I wasn't willing to budge on this. I looked from one to the other, my big guy and my Prince, and knew all they wanted in this realm or any other was to protect me. Keep me safe. But I didn't need protection. Not all the time at least.

I clung to the idea they wanted to help. They hurt and worried, and that was where all this came from, even if it came out as lecturing and anger. Taking a deep breath, I centered myself before I pushed on. "What's done is done, and it was necessary. You have to accept it and accept I can do what's necessary without being reckless or stupid. When we have limited choices, things we'd normally never do get done. Doesn't mean I like it, or you have to like it, but it does mean it needs to be done, and once done, we move on."

Gareth's tense body held for several beats of silence then deflated as he moved to sit beside me on the couch. "I was so worried," he said.

"I know. So was I."

Ny looked at both of us and nodded. "I need to feel you, sweetling."

I knew what he meant. The anger at them for their anger or hurt with me had leaked out, replaced by need and a desire to reconnect after so much swirling shit. I leaned into him harder. He flinched back slightly, so I immediately stopped.

"I may need a moment," he said, though desire made his eyes all good-spacey. "Gareth, can you?"

Gareth's hands slid up my back and gripped my shoulders, turning me so I faced him. He kissed me deep, our tongues clashing as we just had, but in a far more pleasant way. I wasn't in the mood for soft or sweet, and Gareth gave the perfect amount of hard with the bite of his teeth and the grip of his hands. We all needed to feel, let sensation ride us like worry and stress and fear had for the day, so I leaned into it, moving to straddle his hips and push him to his back. I ground down hard on him, and we moaned into each other's mouths as we each tore at the other's clothes. Our lips ripped apart long enough for us to whip our shirts over our heads. I disconnected my body from his so I could get out of my pants as quickly as possible. Gareth pushed his jeans and boxers down past his hips, letting his erection bounce before he took it in hand and gave himself a hard stroke.

I was already wet and ready, but seeing that made me even more so. I climbed on top, taking him inside in one swift plunge, both of us hissing out our enjoyment. I felt Ny's hands roam my flesh as I ground down onto Gareth. Gareth's hands were at my hips, keeping me locked in place so I couldn't move much more.

I felt Ny's front against my back. His hand brushed the hair off my shoulder, and he said, "Lean forward, sweetling."

As I did, he followed, lying down on me, sandwiching me between the two of them. He wasn't fully naked. His pants were still firmly in place, scraping my lower back and ass in long strokes. His chest was bare, the heat and power of him draped across my back as Gareth's different but no less delicious warmth seeped into my front.

My body was a livewire, ready to burst with the need to release. Gareth took our combined weight like it was nothing and pulsed in quick, short thrusts, grinding on my clit as he barely moved in and out of me.

"I can't. I can't," I said. Chanted. I didn't even know what I couldn't do, but the guys paused long enough to hold me tight, twining both their strong sets of arms around me.

"We have you," Gareth said. They did. Not just here, physically, but in all ways. It could be frustrating, but it was a small price compared to all I got in return.

"Move. Please," I pleaded, and Ny ground down from above, causing Gareth to moan as it pushed him deeper inside me. He countered with an upward tilt of his hips, and the pressure of both of them made me detonate. My body shook from the release, and I cried out with pure relief. Gareth followed soon after, pulsing into me, and Ny finished on top without even taking off his jeans, shuddering against my backside as he trailed kisses across my shoulders. It was quick and a little rough and a little dirty but also freeing and lovely and loving.

After a minute of being pressed tight to Gareth's chest, I said, "I'm a little squished here, guys."

Ny immediately jumped up, pulling me free of Gareth to cradle me in his arms. "Let's clean you up, yes?"

I nodded, too content to add much else until he cupped my cheek in his hand and said, "You saved me, Randy Carter." His heart was there swirling in the stars of his eyes, and I was reminded of what Azathoth asked about my thoughts on Ny, who he was compared to what he'd been, and I was more than certain saving happened in a bunch of different ways, for all three of us.

"I'll do it every time. Now, maybe as a thank you, you can make me a bubble bath."

A deep echo of laughter sounded, a mix of both Ny and Gareth's voices as magic swirled in a cloud around us.

"Anything," Ny replied. He leaned forward to quickly gather and transfer the magic into Gareth, who took it with a peaceful smile before standing and clasping the Outer God's forearms tight.

Still connected to Ny, Gareth looked me up and down, sparks of heat returning to his eyes. He said, "Bath time," with a delicious grumble. Where I'd been thinking lavender and Epsom salt in the tub, I was now hoping all three of us could squeeze in there. It was a huge tub, because Ny liked oversized things, but I wasn't certain it'd fit me and the dudes together. We'd give it a try though. For sure.

I whipped up some luscious cheddar bacon chive scones in Ny's beautiful Aga and made the guys sit to eat before we got on the weirdest conference call ever. I mean, I was happy to only have to repeat the story of yesterday once, but it was odd doing it over the phone. Especially with Merry and Mia jumping in to be all grumbly about every little thing.

All were happy we now knew how to kill Zeus in theory. We'd hammer out the practical later. When I got to the part about the Slender Man lookalike in the hallway, a deep growl ripped through Ny's house before he literally hissed and said, "Yog-Sothoth."

"Your brother?" I was surprised because one, it meant I'd survived yet another encounter with a new-to-me Outer God, and two, because they didn't look anything alike. "Not much of a resemblance there," I muttered.

"Yog-Sothoth has been tangentially connected to a lot of what's gone down," Harley said, her normally silky smooth and deep voice losing some of its usual tone when forced through tiny phone speakers.

"This is true," Ny admitted. "However, I believe he is not involved directly in any of these events. He has his own machinations to attend to, and he avoided his son at all costs in the past. He would not have employed Wilbur in any grand scheme."

Gareth's body stiffed at Wilbur's name, and I reached for his knee under the table and smoothed it over his jean-clad leg.

"You think it's just a coincidence I ran into him?" I asked.

His jaw was hard, and his eyes were swirling darkness. "Yes. It is unfortunate it occurred because my brother is a very dangerous entity, but I do not believe it is more than a simple accident. The fact our sire engaged and staked a type of claim is something else I do not like, but is a good deterrent for Yog. I do not think he has been or will be involved in our current situation."

I was good with trusting Ny on this, as was everyone else. As there wasn't much to rehash after the Yog stuff, our call devolved, and I spent a few minutes being chastised by my sisters. A Carter sister wouldn't miss an opportunity to chastise one of their own.

Harley eventually shut it down when she jumped in with some new info. "Last night I stayed behind at the abandoned building, studied the sigils as you suggested."

"What did you find?" Ny asked, leaning forward as if drawn to the phone on the table.

"They were drawn in standard practice and the construction was not overly complicated, so I should be able to easily replicate them, especially knowing the purpose behind their creation. I easily broke them using Rich's practical method. After breaking them, a spell of erasure worked well, so those particular ones aren't a problem anymore. I did discover a connection to ley lines that could be interesting."

Gareth and Ny both sat up a little straighter.

"What are ley lines?" Merry asked, her tone still a little hard and a lot pissed off despite her curiosity.

Harley answered in a softer voice, "Ley lines hold all the magic in the earth, allow it to move and pulse from location to location in a semi-regular pattern. For the most part, it contains natural magic well, but a small percentage leeches out into the surrounding areas and either dissipates into other things or is pulled and stored. This is where all the magic mages draw on originates. However, mages have never been able to tap directly into ley lines. They hold too much power, and power protects itself. When I was looking around, I found the building where we were was a zone for a number of crossing lines."

"The interstates," Gareth mumbled.

"What?" I asked.

"Not all interstate junctions are ley line crossroads, but many are. Humans don't all know about ley lines, but many can instinctually sense them, and they are often used as intersecting points of travel or commerce," he explained.

"Humans are fascinating," Ny said, sitting back into his royal feline lean. "Your discovery helps us better understand what power Zeus used to create the sigils, Harley. Exceedingly valuable information."

"Do Other Gods normally have the power to tap into ley lines when mages can't?" Mia asked.

"Godhead has its benefits," Ny said, his sly smile only there for me and Gareth. "The magic various gods command is far more powerful than the magic mages can command because it is an internal fount. I am not surprised Zeus found a way to tap into the ley line powers and use them to boost his own spells, as he has no natural gift of spellcraft. The sigils, once created, should be replicable and act as a drain and transfer spell, as long as we have enough initial power to charge the spell."

"Makes sense," Mia said, "but we still have the problem of finding Zeus once all these puzzle pieces are locked in place."

"I'm working on a few theories," Harley said, "but I may need you and Randy to help iron out details."

I was cool with whatever Harley needed me to do or try. "Just tell me when and where."

"I'll be there," Mia said.

I was ready to start wrapping things up. "Okay, so we know a bit more about where and how Zeus is supercharging things, and we know he wants to do this with both me and Ny now."

"Very succinct, sweetling," Ny said with a sharp-toothed grin.

I rolled my eyes at him. "Thanks."

"Anytime, love."

"We good with everything?" Rich asked. He'd been quiet the entire time, so I was surprised he was the one to jump to end the call. Maybe ghouls weren't great with phone convos. Or maybe it was just the generally gruff and quiet Rich.

I answered for everyone, which may have been a little rude, but whatever. "Yep. Everything's straight and we know what we need to focus on now. Harley, text me and Mia when you want to connect. Otherwise, I'll talk to everybody later."

We said our good-byes, and I stared at the black screen on the phone for a few beats after the call ended.

"You really okay, Randy?" Gareth asked, leaning over to put a big mitt of a hand over my own lying on the tabletop.

I shook off my thoughts and smiled at him. "Sure, considering. I'm ready for this to be over. Every time we get an answer to a big question, we come up with another big question, and I'm more than a little sick of it."

"It's the way magical mysteries work sometimes," he said. "I know it's frustrating, believe me. We'll get through and get over."

"Yes, sweetling," Ny said as he rose from his chair. "I have no doubt we will be the victors in this battle of ours."

"How are you so sure?" I asked, needing a little reassurance to bolster me.

He leaned down, smacked a loud kiss on the crown of my head, and said, "Because I've seen us in different times, love. I know we have a stretch of life after this."

It wasn't a whole lot of detail, but I didn't push. Because Ny didn't have the Book of Knowing right then, I often forgot he knew some stuff about the future. Knew of us in the future. It was a comfort, though it made me curious.

"Do you know if you two will ever let me boss you both around in the bedroom instead of always being the growly directors?"

Ny and Gareth both laughed deep and long.

"You have an Outer God here with all kinds of future knowledge, and that's what you want to know?" Gareth asked, shaking his head at me as he also rose from his seat.

"It's a serious question," I huffed, going into fake-pout mode. It was an interesting question, at least. Made my mind turn to better things after the new, darker, and more intense questions we now had hovering after the call.

"Sorry, sweetling. I'll never tell," Ny called to me as he started piling dishes into the dishwasher. Having him around had multiple benefits, but apparently him telling me stuff about our future wasn't one of them. I snorted because it reminded me a little of Azathoth's parting answer to me, but I wasn't about to tell Ny he sounded like his sire. Not many people liked hearing they were like their parents, and I don't think my Prince would be an exception to the rule. Best I kept the observation to myself.

# Twenty

IT WAS TWO DAYS before Harley texted me to come by her place. Or their place. I think at that point Merry was stationed full time at Harley's condo instead of her cute little house. I was all for it because Harley's place was like a magical Fort Knox with all those wards she had in and around it.

I'd become more and more used to shadow walking, so I left my car behind and jumped over there in a few short seconds. Still, I didn't break Harley's wards and bust into her home without letting her know I was there. Would've been plain rude. Instead, I stopped at a shadow in an alley by her house and rang her bell like a regular person.

Harley took me straight to the library, so I figured Merry was at her office at the LGBTQ youth shelter for the day. Mia was there, curled up in the big comfy chair and flipping through an old book. She looked up as I entered and smiled. For the first time in a long time, her face held shades of the old Mia—a bit of sly snark and happiness and intelligence all mixed in with the tilt of her head, the curve of her lips, and the light of her eyes. There was something extra there when I looked at those dark-brown eyes more closely, something moving around inside her that she hadn't had before. Not what I would've ever wanted for my baby sister, but she was handling things well, so it was better than before. Much better, and part of me knew without asking Rich helped her get to this place, which made me even more thankful the ghoul had decided to come back to our realm.

"Sup, sis?" she asked, closing the book in her hands before thumping it down on the side table and stretching tall in her seat. Or as tall as her petite frame allowed.

"Not much. You know, the usual: plotting on how to kill an ancient Greek god and honing my powerful magic skills. You?"

"Oh, nothing new. Learning how to harness the awesome power of the magical book permanently planted in my brain."

Harley snorted behind me, then skirted around to stand on my other side, creating an easy triangle with her at the apex, once again leaning against her work desk with her arms folded on her chest. It's like it was the only way she could stand, seriously. But I had to admit, it made her look both hot and badass, what with the smooth nonchalance of it all and the flexing forearm sigil tats on full display, so why mess with a good thing? I was sure Merry appreciated the hell out of it, much like I internally drooled a bit when Gareth did his wide-legged feet planting thing or Ny did his regal, loose-limbed lounge.

"As entertaining as your Carter banter can be," Harley drawled, "we have business to discuss."

"The business of magical books and godlike powers, which is what we were actually discussing," Mia said, leaning back and flashing a saccharine-sweet smile. Good to see she shined her little-sister attitude at others also.

I strolled over to rest my butt on the arm of the chair where Mia still sat and folded my own arms over my chest. "Okay, Harley. We're all serious now. What's up?"

She straightened from her lean. "What's up is Mia may have discovered a way to track Zeus."

Flashing a smile over my shoulder at Mia, I said, "Nice," but let them fully explain before I jumped in too much.

"Rich and I've been working on accessing more of the Necronomicon. When I use it, it soothes the thing somehow, and it stops trying to dominate my mind. I still can't access all of it, but I'm learning more and more every day. Harley here asked me to direct my intention."

"She's big on that," I quipped, then shut up so Mia could continue.

"Sure is. Anyway, if I think about a very specific thing long enough, and the book has some type of answer, it will eventually show it to me."

"You're saying the book gave you a spell to track Zeus?"

"Not Zeus per se, but to track gods in an area."

"Okay. How do we kickstart this magical GPS system?"

"I already have most of it done," Harley answered, motioning me to follow her as she moved to a folding table now situated right in the middle of the room, in the sliver of space between where the library ended and the training area began. I hadn't thought anything of it when I came in, but as I moved closer, I got the distinct taste of new magic, something like a mixture of Harley's clove with the musty smell of old paper. A map of Columbus lay on the table, unrolled and held in place by heavy, smooth gray stones, each with a different sigil on it.

"I take it you need me to finish."

"You or Ny, but we'd like to try you first. I've gotten more used to the Prince—we're on good terms—but I'm still not about to ask him for blood before exhausting our other options."

"Blood?"

"Yep." Mia came to stand in the line we had facing the map. "We need a drop of blood from a god."

Staring at both of them, I stated what I thought was obvious. "I'm not a god."

Harley shook her head at me. "Come on, Randy. You have an Other God's recycled powers, and they grow every day. You're as close to a god as a human can get."

"'As close to' is an important distinction. Probably even more important for godly spells and shit."

Mia pressed her hand over mine, which I realized was tensed in a fist. "Randy, you can do this."

I closed my eyes. I'd had some realizations with Azathoth, sure. Was coming to terms with my magic and the fact I was randomly chosen or whatever, but this would be tangible proof of my difference if it worked. More so than Ny's flute trick because it'd leave a visible piece of something behind. Something I, or anyone else for that matter, could point at and say, "Look, you're not actually human." I was handling all this new shit well, but this was a big step.

"Randy," Harley called, forcing me to look at her. "We can ask Ny. Or you can ask Ny, because I don't really want to, but that's not the point. We don't absolutely have to use your blood. Mia is certain it will work, and both of us think it might be good for you to try."

"You've been nosy little biddies talking about me then?" I asked on a huff.

"Look, Randy. I love you. I trust you. You saved me in a completely different realm, for fuck's sake. Even before all the magic-book business, you were my big sis, one of the few people on this earth who I knew would always have my back, would always fight like hell for me. I wouldn't ask you to do this if I thought it wouldn't work. I definitely wouldn't ask you to do this if I thought it would hurt you. For real, Randy. I think it will help you and help us all."

Then Harley dropped a truth bomb with a shrug of her shoulder. "The only thing holding back your power is your brain telling you there are limits to your power. I think—we think—if you see it activate a god spell, you may just prove to yourself you can do so much more."

"We need more, Randy, if we want to actually take out Zeus for good."

They were right, damnit, but it didn't mean I wasn't scared. That was really what it came down to in the end. Me being scared of what I was, what I could do, what I might become.

I whispered a question in the silence of the room. "What if I lose myself?"

Mia squeezed the hand she still held. "You won't, Randy, because you're a badass and always have been. But if you do, we'll bring you back. We'll fight like hell to get you back to us."

Mia had tears at the corners of her eyes as she said it, and I believed her, because I'd done the same for her and I knew she loved me with the exact same ferocity.

I relaxed my jaw, unlocked my tense muscles, and leaned into my much-littler sister. She took my weight and held me, giving me even more assurance in her light touch. "You got this, sis," she whispered in my ear as she gave my dark hair a quick, soft stroke. I looked over at Harley to see her nodding in her stern but sure way. Neither of these strong-as-hell women doubted me, so why should I doubt myself?

"How much blood do you need? We talking a syringe worth or a bucket full?"

Harley chuckled. "We need a single drop, released over the map."

"What happens if it works?"

"Well, theoretically, we should be able to view, then track, the location of all the gods in the map's area."

"Might tell us more than we want to know," I muttered and both Mia and Harley nodded their agreement.

"Okay, what do I do?"

According to them, it was pretty simple. I needed to hold my hand about a foot above the table, cut my finger with a silver blade, and let a single drop fall somewhere over the middle of the map. Then, magic. Blowing out a big breath, I moved quickly to get it over with. Harley gave me a wicked-sharp silver blade from the training area, which she'd disinfected with an alcohol wipe. Safety first, even in magical rituals. I pricked my finger with the tip, and a small smear of blood appeared. My hand hovered over the map as I pushed up my pointer finger with my thumb, making the blood well and eventually drop in a small, wobbly circle over the map.

It didn't drop onto the map. A few inches above the thing, the droplet stopped midair, quivering there for a second as I worried it'd fail. Then it spread out in a thin, barely visible red haze before softly floating to encase the map. The paper flashed red before it dimmed back to normal. Well, normal except for the three tiny bright-red dots hovering above different spots on the map. One was in the Short North, showing where I stood in Harley's condo. Another was off to the east, hovering around Ny's place in German Village. The third, the one we really needed, was centered downtown, almost right between my and Ny's dots. Given its location, it was probably the apartment I'd visited when I'd first seen Zeus here in Columbus.

Mia let out a whoop of excitement and hugged me. Harley, ever her stoic self, gave me a quick, hard pat on the back and leaned over the map. I was a little all over the place emotionally. I guess it proved I was godlike enough for a spell, but I was unsure how it would help me in the way Mia and Harley were sure it'd help.

"Looks like we don't have any god surprises, at least," Mia said as she studied the map.

"Some good news for a change," I said.

Harley was busy studying the map but managed to mutter some words. "Thanks, Randy. This will be very helpful once we have a solid plan of attack in place," Harley said.

"It'll stay like this, tracking wherever the three of us are?"

"As long as no one moves these sigil stones," Harley answered.

"Good. Need anything else from me?"

"Not immediately, but—"

"Then I'm out," I said, cutting Mia off.

"We need to discuss potential plans," Harley insisted.

"Later," I said, already moving toward the door. "I need to do some stuff on my own first."

They didn't try to stop me or anything, which I was thankful for. I had a lot of things knocking around in my head, and I needed space to think. I also suspected I needed alone time to explore. Maybe I also needed to experiment a little more with a magic I'd only learned about recently, which meant I needed to go to the one place I knew I might be able to tap into ley lines. I'd just confirmed I was for sure godlike, if not fully godly, so it was time I started acting a little more like a god and got shit done.

# Twenty One

The broken-down business looked exactly the same, except the Writhing and the toasted bodies of the mages were gone. Oh, and the sigils were broken, their magic made ineffective by strategic scrapes across the paint. The magic was also gone, the smell and taste dissipating somewhere. I wasn't about to be stupid. I popped my spear into existence, so I was ready for anything to come at me in the space.

I stood there a few minutes, taking in the mostly empty scene and thinking back to what had happened here and what Zeus might have planned. Ultimately, though, rehashing what Zeus did to me wasn't why I went back there. I went back to explore my magic, connect to my godhood or whatever and come to terms with my shit on my own. I'd been doing my usual ostrich thing, trying to ignore all the implications of what I'd unlocked in the Dreamlands, only dealing with what was right in front of me, only exploring when the people around me asked me to try something new. It was passive as hell, and after this afternoon with Mia and Harley, I knew a personal one-on-one between me, myself, and I—and my magic—was truly in order. I needed to consciously try to connect with and learn from the godly power inside me, the thing that'd made me different from birth. If I didn't, I couldn't fight Zeus. Plain and simple. What I could learn about myself, my power, and the past was necessary so we could get things sorted in the present. No more hiding. I was facing it all.

I wandered the space, thinking through my options, and decided I needed to go old school. Go back to the first bits of magic I ever knew to see what it now held. I hadn't returned to the shadow realm in weeks and weeks, and it well could have changed in my time away or with my increase in power. I centered myself, thought of the shadow realm, and took a small step forward, slicing through the human realm and stepping foot into the same space but in a different place.

It was all grayscale, as per usual. However, there were traces of glow around, magical energy I couldn't see in the human realm. The spear in my hand also shimmered, the magic of the object itself echoing in the shadow realm like Ny had. I heard the faint slithering of things in the distance, creatures attracted to my magic for whatever reason, and fear spiked in me for a moment before I twisted the spear, willing it away so the torch of monster-repellant light Ny taught me replaced it. The flames glowed and flickered and the sounds stopped, leaving me in gray silence.

Standing in the center of the room, I was a little lost for what to do next. Magic pulsed in me, hard and deep and fast. I felt comfortable in this place for the first time in a long time, much like I had when I was a kid and I played there. My magic shielded me from the things I'd come to fear, which gave me time to explore. Eventually I studied the sigils and their fading glow and traced the line of waning magic with my eyes, watching it stretch up in beats and whirl back down into the concrete. Zeus had placed them where he could draw or manipulate the most power, so they had to be the points where ley lines intersected in the space.

I circled, counting five total sigils marking the concrete, all with faint magical glows hovering on or around them. They had to be where the ley lines crossed. It didn't give me much beyond location, but maybe location could be enough. I moved to kneel by the closest sigil again, reaching my free hand out to run my fingers through the magic twirling above it. The soft tendrils weren't shadows, a thing I was used to commanding. They glowed a bright white and looked like smoke curling from a cigarette. When I touched them, they reacted kind of like DD did, jumping and twining with my hand, interacting with me. They tasted of fresh gardens and earth and summer sky. They tasted natural and true, realer and more grounded in the human realm than any of the other magic I'd sensed in the last few months.

A phantom tug pulled my hand down to the cold concrete. I followed the magic's lead and placed a hand on the broken sigil as the smoky light whirled around my hand and up my arms. There was a gentle nudge against my palm, a request to enter, and I opened for it mentally, inviting it in and letting this new type of magic flow into me.

I should've braced, because as soon as I opened myself up to it, power slammed through me, flowing in what felt like an endless wave, a brimming... a filling up like a too-stuffed eclair. It was literally the opposite of what I'd experienced there before. No drain, no taking, only giving and opening. I couldn't rightly say how long I kneeled there, hand glued to the floor and pulsing with the magical power entering my body. Could've been seconds or it could've been hours. I know at some point I blacked out or blanked, because one moment I was being filled with this smoky, earthy magic and the next I was lying cold on the concrete floor, back in the human realm well past dark as the building was filled with evening shadows and the weak light of streetlamps.

I bolted upright, rubbing my slightly numb hand and looking around for my torch or any other protection. Didn't find it, not even DD hovering in sight. Instead, I saw a voluptuous woman in a black robe, holding a spear in one hand and examining her wicked-long, sharp nails with the other. She was hazy, not fully solid, but she was definitely there.

"I was worried you would never wake," she said as I stared at her, my mouth hanging open in surprise. She offered a hard smile, like it was something she rarely gave out, and her face was so gorgeous it almost hurt to look at her. She was all smooth, tanned skin and voluptuous curves, slightly less fluffy than my midsize frame. Her regal nose, full pink lips, and sharp cheekbones mixed to form an achingly beautiful face. Dark-brown hair, not as dark as mine but damn close, formed a crown of curls on top of her head. She was gorgeous in a way I'd never seen before, but her eyes were like most of the gods I'd encountered so far: dark and unreadable with fathomless depths.

"Hecate?" I whispered. Who the hell else could it be? She had my robe on and my spear in her hand. Or her things I now had, whichever way I wanted to think about it.

"Of a sort," she said, giving me a small bow of her head.

Her answer snapped me out of my amazement and post-magical weirdness stupor. Mostly because it pissed me right the hell off. Damn these gods and their constantly cryptic bullshit.

"Cut the crap," I said with an exhausted sigh. "Obviously you know who I am. You probably also know what's going on. How about you save us both the time and annoyance and just say whatever it is you came here to say."

She cracked out a laugh, loud but rusty, and it rang out in the nearly empty space. "Oh, I can see why my magic was drawn to you."

I stood, cocked a hip, and rolled my hand in the universal gesture for her to get on with it as she smiled her sharp-toothed smile at me. "I am not exactly Hecate. Not all of me. I am the small part still attached to my power."

"You, like, know what she knew and all that?"

"Yes, Randy."

My stance relaxed at her calling me by my preferred name. She was the first god to do so without me asking. Ny hadn't even done it at first. It was a small thing in the grand scheme of magic and shadow and god business, but it was important to me. Important enough I felt more comfortable in her presence.

"You're kind of chilling inside me with my magic?"

"Something like that, though not fully, and not for much longer. I have spent all my available energy to visit you in this way."

"You killed yourself to talk to me," I said deadpan, disbelieving for a moment.

"In so many words, but as you know, energy doesn't end. Not really. My power is in you, as you know. These last remnants I called my own will dissipate, likely flowing into the ley lines here, becoming something else, something new. I am at peace with this. You are an acceptable vessel for my power here in the human realm."

I snorted at her not-so-glowing endorsement but pushed on to the real point. "Okay then. What's so important you decided to change your energy to have a chat?"

"Zeus must be stopped."

"No shit."

Her eyes went onyx hard at the sarcasm, but she visibly shook it off and continued without commenting. "You've bumbled into tapping into the ley lines, which is good, but you have no idea how to use them. How they can help you drain, then kill Zeus."

"And?" I was really hoping she'd be blunt and up front, simply giving me what I needed without much fuss.

Her form wavered and I took a quick step forward to try to catch her or hold her or something. Her face pinched a moment, and she tilted her head at me, shining black circles bouncing around as she did. "No time to talk. Only to show."

I huffed out a breath and said, "Okay, fine, but this better not be a big old mystery I can't figure out, or your whole gambit was pointless."

She didn't answer with words. Her spear hand shot out, not to cut but to tap me, like she was a queen dubbing me a knight, moving from my left to my right shoulder. At the last whisper-soft touch of the spear point, I felt a jolt, the world lost focus, and suddenly I was in a grassy field somewhere, watching as Zeus and Hecate argued a dozen yards away. I couldn't hear them, but I could see them. Hecate was pacing, shaking her head, her face showing her obvious annoyance. Zeus appeared placating but condescending, as per usual. When it looked like Hecate would turn away from him, he stopped her with a hand on her shoulder, moving her ever so slightly as he leaned in to whisper something. The whisper felt harsh and more than a little creepy, even from my removed place in this vision or whatever. The creep vibes certainly matched Hecate's reaction. Her tanned face lost all color, and she violently shook off Zeus's hand. As she backed up slowly, her down-turned mouth shot words at Zeus, words which made even the cocky god flinch, though only for a second.

Zeus recovered and offered a truly insincere smile. A smile which grew bolder and broader when she went to make another step but was locked in place. He raised some electricity, a white-hot light unlike the usual blue sparks he used, and in an instant she was floating, doing basically the same thing I'd done in the sigil. I hated to watch, because I knew where it was going. She fought. She screamed. She probably cursed the stupid and cruel god in front of her. Until she didn't anymore, and her body went limp and loose.

Zeus brought her body to the ground, laying her crumpled and shivering at his feet. He stepped up, offering a hand, but she smacked it away with the little energy she seemed to have, whispering some words that made his face harden even more. In response, he filled her with his blue lightning, burning her like he did his mages. It took longer, and he did a more thorough job, but her body eventually turned to ash and blew in the soft wind, scattering through the field. Zeus blinked, his shoulders losing some tension with a small slump, and turned to leave, walking right by me as he did.

He didn't see me, of course. Or the even more ghostly form of Hecate at my side.

"Pretty straightforward," I muttered to her. "He used the ley line power to drain you, then help him destroy your weakened body, right? I'll have to do the same, right? Mix my power, Zeus's lightning, and the ley line power to have enough umph to make him completely disappear?"

She didn't speak, probably couldn't with all the energy she'd used to literally show me the damn thing, so she gave a hard, quick nod of her head. It was not far off from what we already knew, but the little extra bit about process, about combining, was important. Probably crucial. And I wouldn't have had it unless Hecate had sacrificed what was left of herself inside me to let me see what had gone down.

"I get it," I said to her before I reached to try to hold her hand. It wasn't really there, and neither was I because this was all some projected-memory thing, but I wanted to comfort and reassure her. "I know what I need to do now."

On the wind I heard a single word. "We."

"Yes. We. Us. All of us. We got this. You don't need to worry about it anymore."

She reached up to try to stroke my face. Her eyes shimmered black in her hazy outline, and I saw the ghost of a tear trickle down her face. My heart hurt for her, this goddess taken out by an asshat god. I didn't know her, not really, but I knew her magic. Used it every day now. Felt her as a part of what made me *me*, so I couldn't help but feel for her.

Her ghostly form moved down and tapped my chest like a gentle breeze, and my magic thumped hard in response. Her eyes were darkness and pain as she looked back in my face, not having the words to say whatever she wanted to express.

I wasn't 100 percent sure what she needed to tell me, what made her really sad in this moment. She was fading, which would make any being sad. She was also counting on me to get some serious stuff done, and not knowing the outcome would've also likely hurt. I chose to think she was saying good-bye to her magic, a magic I was certain was now my responsibility. My heart hurt for her, watching the last bits wavering where she stood, and I whispered past the lump in my throat, "I got you."

She closed her eyes as if pained and flickered in and out of sight. My vision did the same until, in a blink, I was back to the dark building, watching as Hecate faded more and more from view. I gave a sad wave her way and she raised her spear, her final smile a touch feral and her eyes hard as she did. She'd get her revenge, even if she wasn't around to see it. I'd deliver for her, for myself, for Deb. For everybody I knew and all the people I didn't. Thanks to the spark of Hecate deep inside she released or let go of or whatever, I knew how we'd do it.

# Twenty Two

"Seems suspect," Harley mused as she paced the gleaming hardwood of her mage lair.

"Just because you have a healthy suspicion of all things godly doesn't mean they're all actually out to get us. Or Randy," Merry said. As Harley strolled near, she stopped her and pulled her to stand still at her side.

"I'd usually agree with Harley," Gareth said, looking at each person gathered in the space, "but with what you said about the events earlier in the day and Randy's descriptions, I lean more toward believing at this point."

Ny nodded. "I knew Hecate. She was straightforward, for a god. I do not believe she would lead Randy astray."

"Are we sure it was actually Hecate or some form of her and not a trick from Zeus?" Rich asked.

"I felt it was her. Plus, I didn't detect any ozone smell, which is a dead giveaway for Zeus," I answered.

"Good enough for me," Mia said, stepping up to rub her hand along my back. Everyone else agreed, although Harley looked a little skeptical when she did.

"Time to plan then," I said, clapping my hands and turning to face Harley head-on. "That's kind of your forte, so any ideas?"

Her dark forehead scrunched and her brows folded, her eyes staring through me until her face smoothed and she said, "I have a few ideas."

"Of course you do, babe," Merry said, beaming up at her with her usual happy exuberance. "What do you need from us?"

"I need Gareth's help with the sigils. Some investigating into ley lines around Columbus. And some work with the Necronomicon—with both Mia and Nyarlathotep."

"Gotcha," I said, corralling everyone into agreeing. "I'll work on ley line research with Merry and Rich."

Ny shook his head. "No. They can handle research on their own. Rich's ghoul powers will allow him to sense the magic from ley lines more readily than any human, even a mage." He pointed over at the training portion of the room. "You need to practice attempting to recreate the power you saw Zeus use on Hecate."

"Smart," I muttered before giving a chuckle. "Harley, you may want to beef up your fire wards real quick before you go off to do something else."

"Most def," she said, walking away to reinforce whatever she needed to reinforce so I could play with pulling together parts of a spell I'd only seen in my weird vision. I had the taste of Zeus's lightning. I also knew the power of the ley lines and could still feel it pulsing in me. Hopefully it was enough to get the job done.

We'd become pretty used to fight prep over the last few months. Everyone had an assignment. Everyone knew the stakes. We all needed to protect each other, and potentially the wider world, from Zeus's hostile takeover. We broke up our usual clutch, and no one wasted time to go about their business and get it done. Seeing these people, many of them strangers until fairly recently, coming together to get shit done, made me all tingly inside. I felt my heart thump hard, not from magic, but from the hope growing more and more steadily in my chest. We had answers, we had direction, and more importantly, we had each other to get it all done. Zeus was toast for sure.

MERRY AND MIA WERE oohing and ahhing over Ny's Aga two days later. Who wouldn't? I'd texted them to come over, take a break from whatever magic stuff they were digging into, and have lunch with me. Like always, there they were, hovering as I pulled the steaming quiche out of the oven. I smelled the cheese and shallots and fresh herbs, tasted the memory of it on my tongue, and thought back to a time when food was all I tasted. No more, but I wasn't too mad about it. I knew this beautifully baked eggy concoction would taste a lot better than the ozone and spark that'd been filling my mouth lately.

I placed the golden quiche on a trivet and moved to the fridge to get out the salad I'd made earlier. It was simple, spinach and field greens with cucumbers, celery, and pepitas mixed in, but I'd also made my own mustardy dressing for it, so I knew it'd be awesome.

I shoved the big bowl in Mia's hands as I shut the fridge door with my hip. "Here, be useful."

She wrinkled her nose at me but put the salad on the mostly empty dining table close to the kitchen. I didn't say anything to Merry. She picked up the stack of plates and forks on the counter and followed Mia from the kitchen as I riffled through drawers.

"Yes," I hissed, holding the pie server I'd found in the back of a drawer up high like it was Excalibur.

"There's no way Ny had that thing in his kitchen just randomly," Mia said with a scoff.

"Of course it wasn't random. He had it for Randy," Merry said, smiling brightly at me as she did.

She was right. There was no reason the Outer God needed a shiny, silver pie server. Not only had I never seen him cook or grab food on his own, I'd never actually seen him eat unless he was sitting down to eat a meal with me. No random snacking, no talk of grabbing food because he was hungry. It was an odd thought, the idea Ny didn't need to eat but only did it for me. To be with me in those small moments.

"Someone's thinking hard," Mia said. She was already seated, pulling a big clump of salad from the bowl to plop down on the plate placed in front of her.

"Yes. Please. Help yourself," I called, snatching up the hot egg pie with oven mitts and carrying it to the table with the pie server stabbed in the middle. I carefully cut three big slices and opened my palm in the universal gimme gesture at each sister. Both passed their plates, and mine, so I could fill it with cheesy eggy goodness. "Don't start scarfing right away," I said to Mia, who already had a forkful hovering toward her mouth. "Let it cool a bit first. Jeez."

"Sorry," she said, putting her fork down and folding her hands in front of her like she was patiently waiting for the exact moment she could eat. I teased Mia about it, but I hadn't actually seen her eat like this in a while. It felt good, to give her food I'd made and have her joy and excitement be so obvious.

"Go ahead," I said, waving my hand at her. "Have at it."

We all dug in, the sound of forks hitting stoneware the only noise for a few minutes. Merry finally broke the happy silence of chowing down with "this is great, sis" before she took another big bite of her quiche.

"Yep," Mia said around her own mouthful.

"Thanks. I've thought about making quiche at Warm Regards but don't know if I want to dip my toe into more savory stuff just yet."

Mia's dark eyes met mine and she asked, "How's the work going?"

I shrugged. "I've been a little preoccupied with other stuff, but I do still talk to the contractor occasionally. Because of their previous schedule, and the fact the job involves so many different types of things, like matching brick work and replacing pipes and electrical and whatnot, it's taking a while. He was upfront about it though, so it's what I expected. As of now, they've started, and it won't be done for a few more weeks."

Mia's head dipped, and I put my fork down to reach for her. "Hey. You know you don't have to go back there, right?"

She squinted her eyes at me and asked, "Why would I not go back there? I loved the place nearly as much as you."

Merry knew where I was coming from, all the sister worry and need to reassure also banging around in her somewhere. "Mia, a very traumatic event happened there. It may be best if you stay away for a while, take it easy on yourself."

"Like Randy did?" she shot back, leaning back in her chair and crossing her arms. "If she can go back there, so can I."

I put my hands up. "Okay, Mia. We're just letting you know you don't have to if you don't want to."

She muttered, "I will," and I left it at that, not wanting to push her. She was a grown-ass woman who could make her own decisions, or at least I tried to remind myself of the fact she was all grown even when I still occasionally nagged her like she wasn't.

"Will Rich come around too?" Merry asked, being not at all sly about changing the subject.

"You've been hanging out with him. You can ask him," Mia said, holding on to her sulk a little longer.

"Rich is a good dude. I think." I wanted to know what was going on with Rich and Mia too, but I wasn't going to be overly blunt about the questioning when she'd just shot down our convo about Warm Regards.

She squinted hard at both of us. "Ask what you want to ask, cowards."

I laughed. "Fine. What exactly is up with you and Rich?" I waggled my eyebrows at her in an exaggerated way. "And, for my own personal curiosity, can he take care of business like I imagine he can? He's a big, strapping ghoul, after all."

Merry had been taking a drink of water when I asked this and nearly choked on her laughter. "Yeah, Mia. What's a ghoul like in bed?"

"Rich is complicated, but so am I now. We do just fine in the bedroom, thank you very much. Outside, stuff is a little more nebulous."

"No definitions, no pressure?" I asked, prodding a bit further.

She shrugged. "There's a lot of stuff swirling still, a lot that's uncertain. Until it becomes a little clearer, I don't know if I want to define anything." She was quiet for a moment, lost in her own thoughts. "He left the human realm for the Dreamlands once. I don't even know if he wants to stick around longer than he feels like he has to."

Mia's face was droopy, her eyes a little lost. I wanted this to be a more lighthearted meal, so I let her alone with the Rich business. I knew what it was to feel uncertain about relationship status and futures. I knew, like me, Mia'd find the way for herself and she'd be happy. I believed we all would be happy, one day. I had to, for my own sanity. Still, I felt a little more banter was in order, and there was one sister present who was more secure in her relationship and could take some ribbing.

"You and Harley are practically living together now. Big step, Merry."

She smiled, ready for any teasing we might give her with her usual good-natured attitude. "Harley's awesome and I'm not even a little sad about any of it."

"Will we be looking for white dresses soon?" Mia asked in her fake-sweet sister voice, her tone lifting again.

I barked out a laugh at the idea. "One white dress, very flowy. One suit. Or, ooh, maybe a tux."

Merry propped her head on her hand and stared off. "Harley would look yummy in a tux."

"No lie," Mia and I both said at the same time and laughed. I got "jinx" out first, and she promised to buy me a soda before I let her talk again.

"No wedding bells in the immediate future. At least, none we've talked about yet." She turned shrewd eyes my way. "Don't think you're getting out of this convo."

"Oh, I'll tell you anything you want to know. I'm happy with my dudes the way we are. I love them, they love me, and we even had hot sex over by the desk earlier today. Want the details?"

They laughed, I laughed, and while I didn't tell them everything, I told them enough to have us cackling as we finished our lunch. It was what we needed: time to ourselves, time to talk about everyday things like love and sex and dating and hope for a bright future. Time away from the shitstorm we were about to plow right into with Zeus. Carter-sister time.

# Twenty Three

It was a game of tag, really. That was what I told myself as I stood on one of the grassy hills in Franklin Park, only a short car ride or shadow walk away from Zeus's previous ley line hideout, shaking out my hands and flexing my fingers. I saw the flare of purplish light about fifty yards off, the smell of clove hitting my nose right after signaling Harley had her ward in place. She and Gareth would shore it up however long this took so no random dog walkers busted in on a godly fight scene or got hit by a stray bolt of lightning. Hopefully it wouldn't take long. DD sent nervous energy down our line, matched by its shaking body beside my left eye. "It's all good, my dude," I cooed aloud. Saying it didn't make either of us feel better, but it was still good to say.

The plan was basic because sometimes simpler was better. Everyone had a part to play. Well, everyone had an active part to play except Merry. Her lack of magic made her an easy target in a fight, which is what we all had told her when we begged her to stay far away, safe and guarded behind the wards at Harley's condo. She was having none of it, eventually looking from me and Mia to Harley and whispering, "Everyone I love will be there. In danger. You can't ask me to sit back and not know." I had been ready to stand my ground, having dealt with the puppy-dog looks and soft voices she used when laying it on thick, but I'd watched Harley slump, her resolve crumbling in real time. Our compromise: Merry sat in her now-warded car in a lot farther away but still in the park so she could get here if someone called her. I imagined her clutching her phone in her hand, waiting for a call to come and hoping one didn't all at once. Not a nice mental picture, but it made me grit my teeth and get started. We all needed this done.

I looked at the map at my feet. It'd been real awkward getting this paper map here while making sure the stones stayed in place without anything for the map or stones to solidly sit on. We managed it eventually, thanks to Rich's quick ghoul reflexes and a stabilization spell Gareth knew. Which was good, because we needed updated info from the spell, so it was the only way. My dot blinked right where I was. Ny's dot was steps inside where I knew Harley's ward descended around the designated space. Zeus was still downtown, not physically far from where I stood.

I left everyone behind as I dipped into the spell threads of the map, teasing them with my tongue and feeling them out so I could follow one thread direct to Zeus, like I'd done the first time I visited his fancy-schmancy apartment overlooking the Scioto River.

He was startled, literally jumped a good two inches, when I popped into his house, dressed in my usual Hecate astral-projection garb. He'd been doing gods-knew-what, but I'd caught him in mid-stride, moving across his shiny and cold living room, away from his wall of windows. He was impeccably dressed in a gray-sky suit with an electric-blue tie, which seemed to be his standard look in the human realm. Not a gray hair on his head or short beard was out of place, even when his body reacted to my surprise visit.

"Sup?" I asked, crossing my arms and giving him a big, fake smile.

"What are you doing here?" His question was a demand, hints of astonishment mixed with the indignation in his voice. He stood taller after the question, straightening the lapel of his jacket as he did like it was some armor protecting him.

"We need to have a little chat. I'm tired of this back-and-forth business. You want to take over the human world with your little James-Bond-villain-level plan or whatever, and you know by now I can't let you do it. Why keep dancing around together? We know where each other stands. I say we fight it out now."

He looked me over, sizing me up, likely calculating his odds based on whatever new plan he had brewing at the moment. He didn't say anything, so I continued.

"You can choose where. It needs to be now though. I have other shit to do, you know."

A predatory grin hit his lips. "Very well," he said with a drawl. "I accept your terms; however, can I have more time to prepare? I know a place where we will not be disturbed, but arrangements must be made."

I shrugged. "As long as it's today."

He eyed me, probably suspecting today was important. It was, but not because of the day but for what I knew had to happen.

"I need an address, a time. Something here," I said into the silence, letting impatience bleed into my voice.

Zeus didn't like it much, if the tick in his jaw was anything to go on. He strolled to a small desk against the far wall across from his floor-to-ceiling windows. "It is in what you call the Worthington area," he said as he wrote.

Like the business he'd picked before, Worthington was an area where a number of smaller highways, bypasses, and interstates intersected in spots, making it a likely place for ley-line activity. He was predictable as hell, which is what I was banking on in this whole thing.

He stepped close to me, a condescending tilt to his head as he said, "I will meet you in three hours. No sooner."

I reached for the paper he extended between two fingers toward me but bypassed it, instead clasping hard on the sliver of wrist exposed beneath his suit. "I changed my mind," I said with a feral grin. "I think we'll do this now." In a blink, I wrapped Zeus's own transport spell around him, the one he'd failed to use properly on Mia weeks ago. After long hours of spellcraft practice, I knew it'd work for me. I pushed all my shadow power into it and called him back with me to Franklin Park.

I was back in my body in a flash, and Zeus lay crumpled at my feet right on top of the map. Good thing we didn't need it anymore. He roared and bounced up, hitting me with a sucker punch to the jaw as he did. My chin exploded in pain, which radiated up my face as the impact shook the bones in my skull. I wasn't used to taking hits to the face, and it hurt like hell. I blinked rapidly but not rapidly enough to have my bearings before Zeus tackled me to the ground.

My back hit hard, slamming the wind out of my body. I struggled to breathe as the god hovering above me punched me in the face one, two, three times more, each hit a shock to the system, each impact making the back of my head connect with the ground with a smack. I don't know why I hadn't thought of this possibility. Why none of us had. Zeus was a god with lots of power, sure, but he also had fists, and they fucking hurt.

Luckily, DD zipped in between us as the man reared back for a fourth hit, creating a solid shadow shield between me and the very angry god guy. Zeus hit DD, making it shake, but it was physical force, not magical, and DD could easily hold its own. I took a beat to catch my breath, shake my head clear despite the pounding pain, and refocus. First, I bucked, now thinking beyond the pain of punches and feeling nauseated at the way the guy was straddling me on the ground.

He tumbled backward, off balance because he'd let his anger control his actions and continued to hit DD instead of gathering his magic or focusing on something else. I scrambled to a crouch, then my feet, flashing the spear into existence to give myself access to its power. I couldn't say the idea of stabbing the dude right then didn't cross my mind. I couldn't do it, because there was a definite plan in place, but I really, really wanted to see him bleed.

My own blood trickled down my face, gushing out of what I then realized was a broken nose. I'd never actually had a broken nose before, but it hurt my face to breathe through it, so I figured that was what it was. Sliding a hand across my lip to get some of the blood out of the way and stop the distracted leaking feeling, I stared hard at Zeus.

"What have you done?" he hissed out.

"Gave you back your own spell, bitch. Thought that was pretty damn obvious. Looks like I did it right, unlike you. Sad, really."

He roared again, his voice echoing thunder as he raised sparks around his clenched fists. Flinging his hands toward me, I moved as quickly as I could, attempting to dodge the blow. He managed to zap a section of DD's shield with a huge bolt of blue lightning, making the power spark and crackle around it. I felt it quiver and shake, tense, then relax as the power slid off again. It held but wouldn't hold up to it very long. DD was great in a fight, but it could get hurt with direct magical hits just like any of us.

Annoyance, fear, pain, and anger were all bubbling up in me now. I shot out with the spear, lashing with shadows in the whip move I'd practiced since my fight with Zeus in the abandoned business, and smacked the Other God with a crack of hard shadow in a diagonal across his broad chest. The suit was singed, blackened, and his skin split, leaving a line of blood where it ripped open. Zeus stumbled back on a foot and looked down like he was mesmerized by the sight of his own blood.

"You dare—"

"Make you bleed? Yeah. No shit. You going to do something about it?"

He raised his hands toward the sky and dark clouds swirled, forming a small tornado funnel over his head. A sneer and a flick of his wrist, and he sent the tiny twister my way. I couldn't move in time and was flung up in the air, then back a good ten feet and once again hit the ground with a hard slap. My back already felt like it was blooming with bruises, and my body ached from all the hits I'd taken. I propped myself up on my elbows, watching as the funnel cloud hovered about five feet away, between me and the Other God.

"Your insolence grows tiring," he said, though his words lacked the normal snide disdain. There was hate there, but it was more heated, filled with anger and a smidge of fear. It made me smile. I wanted him afraid. I was afraid and scared of a lot of shit, including how well the plan would or wouldn't work. He deserved to feel a little fear too.

"I think I will break your body first. It is so fragile. So human still. Then I'll take you away and drain your power. By the end, you'll be begging for death. I'll be merciful and give it to you. However, I will wait. Wait for you to watch as I drain and kill Prince Nyarlathotep, then the Necronomicon. Slit the throats of the mages and your sweet human sister and the stray ghoul as you watch their blood cover my floor. Then I will allow you death."

He walked toward me as he gave his little speech, each step pushing the small wind funnel closer to me. When wind started to whip too harshly, DD came back as a shield, taking the brunt of the miniature blowing storm for me so I could stay planted where I was. I scrambled to my feet, staring and shaking, my knees bent and arms up as if ready to fistfight again. To be fair, it hadn't technically been a fistfight. It was the Other God beating the shit out of me. I'd been through a lot since tapping into my powers long months ago, but Macy was still the only person I'd physically fought. I wasn't sure I could hold up to Zeus, and I didn't really need to, as long as things went according to plan and Zeus kept coming for me.

He had no sneer, no sly smile. Nothing. His face was cold and blank as he talked about killing the people I loved and making me watch. I stood still, taking in his words and growing angrier by the second until my vision turned black, and I knew my eyes went all starry space, like they sometimes did.

Zeus paused and gave an empty smile. "It will be a pleasure to kill a part of Hecate once again," he said, moving to take a step closer, to close the gap between us so he was mere feet away. But he couldn't. He and his magic had reached the end of his tether, and he didn't even know it.

"Funny you should mention Hecate. Had a little chat with what remained of her, and she gave me some very interesting info." I flung my hands out toward the ground, locking onto ley line power, and activated the draining sigil Harley and I had created and disguised under the grass. Zeus's face lost all its smugness and its color before it twisted and his body shot into the air, held in place by the power of the sigil and the ley lines.

# Twenty Four

At that point, I was done. My vision swam in darkness, my face pounded to the beat of my heart, thanks to all those punches to the face, and my magic screamed to be let out, to run roughshod all over the god hovering in the air in front of me. Hecate was supposedly gone, but maybe a bit of her lingered, or her magic remembered, because it really wanted to be let loose on the guy. Couldn't do it though. Not yet. Not until the two people who walked up behind me had their turn with him.

Mia stood back, hugging herself tightly but giving Zeus her most impressive sneer. Ny's eyes locked on mine, then roamed over my face, his starry gazing turning deeper and darker with each sweep of his eyes.

They'd been inside the ward but far enough back to not be detected by Zeus when he landed. Far enough back they hadn't witnessed the punches I took. If Ny's murderous look was anything to go by, my face was already showing the beating, which was not surprising, given the ache in my head.

"You should see the other guy," I said, though it came out a little stiff because my jaw was finding it hard to work.

"Not funny," Mia said, never taking her eyes off Zeus.

Ny said nothing, coming in close to hover a hand over my cheek, barely touching my face. The small whisper of a touch was enough to make me flinch back, and a growl ripped up the Prince's throat. "Oh, sweetling," he said, sorrow and hurt in the dark space of his voice.

"I'll heal," I said with a shrug. "No fun, believe me, but there's more important things to worry about right now."

He gave a curt nod and moved forward a few feet, placing those fathomless nebula eyes on the trapped god in front of us. "We've come for what is ours," he said, his voice a deep boom in the park, the echo odd and chilling seeing as there wasn't anything for it to echo off of in the wide open. He turned toward Mia, who followed his lead and stepped up closer to Zeus.

"I am not afraid." The god had found his bravado, I'd give him that.

Mia sniffed the air as she shook ever so slightly in a whole-body tremor. She was the one not afraid, because something older and stronger and darker was rising under her skin, in her mind, clamoring for its own revenge. "Your scent says different, Zeus." Her voice was somehow deeper, not as echoey as Ny's but leaking force and magic in its own way. Her scent, too, was different. It was hers but with a tinge of something like molded paper and dusty, dark libraries. The Necronomicon was part of her but still something else, something lingering under the surface, waiting to come out.

Mia let it loose. She opened her arms wide and chanted in a language I'd never heard, the words repeating, louder and faster in each pass, until it was a blur of sound I couldn't follow.

Zeus's back bowed, his chest visibly pulling forward and curling back. The smell of book magic I'd detected became stronger, and golden light filtered out of his mouth, nose, and ears. He gasped and shook, but there was no stopping it. Mia... the Necronomicon—one or both or either or whatever—was getting theirs back for the shit he put them through. For the things he'd stolen from them.

The wisps floated out of the sigil, not trapped by the sigil force tuned into godly power, and surrounded my sister, climbing up her open arms and winding their way around her throat. Her head tilted back, and I saw a flash of something else in her eyes from my position beside her before she gasped softly and closed them, opening herself to whatever was there. It flowed in like it had flowed out, through her nose and mouth and ears, filling her up and completing her book, completing her. She stretched up on her tippy toes, almost hovering off the ground, before her body slackened and she folded into a heap on the soft grass.

I moved to her side and knelt to check she was okay, but she was already sitting up.

"I'm good, sis. Promise."

I stayed there beside her but focused back on the Other God and the Outer God. With some info from Harley and Mia's growing access to the Necronomicon, Ny and my sister had found a spell to rip Mia's book's power out of Zeus and filter it back into her. However, Ny was a god like Zeus, could easily be snagged by the sigil. His power, and more importantly the Book of Knowing Zeus had stolen from him along with part of his power, couldn't be busted out without breaking the sigil. We had to get it out of Zeus and find the book and Ny's full power before we drained the Other God, or Ny's power might get sucked out in the process. A tricky maneuver, but one we thought we'd figured out.

Zeus must have realized the magical dilemma as we watched and waited, doing nothing for a short time. He laughed, hollow and harsh, and stared down Ny. "You cannot do the same," he gasped out. "You have no way to harness the Book of Knowing and keep me caged."

Ny shrugged, his body and manner all royal aloofness while his eyes blazed with something much darker. "Maybe not, but we have other ways. First things first."

Ny's shadows spooled out onto the ground and curled at his feet, waiting. Waiting for my own shadows to meet his, to grow and churn and pulse with our combined power as I willed my shadow power outward. It swirled together and moved along the ground like thick black smoke, then stopped at the sigil mark. I'd given my shadows over to DD, who directed them as they moved all around the sigil circle, creating a shadow line outside the draining trap.

Then we waited. It was only a few minutes, but it was a tense few minutes. Mia texted Rich, and he, Harley, and Gareth came bounding up the hill at top speed. Harley's ward of protection was still set, though no longer reinforced. If this didn't work just right, Zeus would blast free, possibly blast out of the ward too, and he'd be wind until he decided to strike again.

Zeus's face scrunched in question, then disbelief, as Harley, a mere mage, knelt in the middle of godly shadow magic and withstood it. She had power he hadn't imagined, but she also had the love and care and trust of me and Ny. Our shadows wouldn't harm her.

Rich came up by Mia's other side, whispered something in her ear, and kissed the hair at the side of her head. He rushed over about twenty feet to the right, one of Harley's wicked-sharp silver blades hovering over an open palm. Gareth stood across from him, and I gave him a weak smile as he took in my face with anger written all over his. His jaw flexed and shoulders bunched with tension, but he said nothing as he took out his own silver knife and mimicked Rich's stance about ten paces across from the ghoul.

"We only have one shot at this," Harley said, bringing my attention back to the circle in front of me.

Ny didn't answer. He closed his eyes, pushing his magic up, infusing it with all his Outer God power. DD followed a half step behind, guiding my power like a general riding into battle. Harley thrust a hand down, her forearms glowing, and a crack sounded as she broke the sigil. At the same instant, the shadow magic flashed into the space, wrapping Zeus in a strong cocoon. Some of Ny's magic reared up like tentacles, circling the god in a tight embrace. They moved up and over, until they extended up from their tight hold around his neck to hover around Zeus's face. The shadow tentacles reared back like a snake and struck him in the eyes. They crackled with dark power, diving deep into his mind.

He opened his mouth to scream, but nothing came out. He shook violently in the air, his head twitching and flopping about as Ny's magic rooted around in his skull. When they pulled back, done digging around for whatever they needed inside Zeus's mind, Ny let out a roar that didn't fit his human shape. It was the same sound he'd made in his lion form when I'd freed him at the black church what now felt like forever ago. A roar of godly triumph.

A hole ripped in time and space above Zeus, and out tumbled a black book, slim and no bigger than my palm. The size was misleading, if the deep thump it made when it hit the ground was anything to go by.

Zeus was struggling to free himself from the shadow, frantic now that Ny had his book back and would soon be his all-powerful self again. "Now, Ny!" Harley yelled, her arms crossed in an X in front of her, sigils flaring.

Ny raced for the book, scooped it up, and tumbled in a smooth ground flip out of the line of fire as Harley blasted Zeus's ass with a green fireball. His body doubled over and went flying when he took the fireball to the stomach, ripping him from the grip of my and Ny's shadow. Rich and Gareth cut their palms at the same time and slapped bloody hands down, saying spell words to complete the second sigil as Zeus flew through the air, making his body bounce off the new sigil's edge before he careened back into the middle space.

"No!" he screamed, his eyes wide and body flailing, trying anything to get free.

"Don't you know, Zeus? Teamwork makes the dream work," I said as I stalked closer, stopping right at the edge of the blood sigil. "Now you're done."

"I'll never be done!" he screamed, spit dripping from his mouth and his face red with rage. "I'm Zeus. I will rule this world again."

I snorted. "You're delusional." I felt a hand at my back and looked over my shoulder and saw Gareth, offering me some of his calm.

"You good with this?" he asked. We all knew what I had to do, but Gareth knew the cost to me. We'd talked enough about death and killing before. I wouldn't really know if I was good with it until I did it, and I had to do it if I wanted to keep me, those I loved, and this whole human world safe from Zeus's grand plans of domination, so I just shrugged and went back to what needed to be done. The touch of calm at my back helped.

Breathing deep, pulling on my new magics, and allowing shadows to swirl inside and fill me, I reached down to the dark inside, using my mind to touch the ley line power speckled in with my shadow now, and called all of it forward and outward. I twisted a hand in the air, Zeus's suspended body following suit, and pulled on the power of the ley line beneath our feet and tucked inside me from my time alone with Hecate, and began to drain the god.

# Twenty Five

Hecate hadn't exactly explained how her power was drained, and the new power we knew Zeus had—his ability to take in the drained power—wasn't clear either. Zeus wasn't about to give us a step-by-step for the process, and he was the only one in existence who we knew for sure had been able to do it. I suppose Azathoth also knew at least some about it, but the King Outer God hadn't given it up, and I wasn't about to track him down and interrogate him. Worst-case scenario, Zeus would be drained and couldn't hurt anyone anymore. Best case, his power would be folded into my own so it couldn't leak out and infect something or someone else, and I'd have the added, and very satisfying, benefit of acquiring the power to fry him to smithereens.

The ace we had was Harley, who'd dug into the sigils we'd found at the abandoned business, working out what was added, what they did, and how they might react to draining and the inclusion of ley line power. She was the brains of this entire operation, had been from the jump, and she used those formidable brains to work out a process. The draining part was simple; it was activated by connecting ley line power inside me to the ley line power beneath the sigil. The kicker, what would give the extra oomph of magical transfer, was to twist my own godly power in with it and use them together to call the combo of ley line power and pull Zeus's power back into myself.

It was the only way we could figure for me to snatch his power. How his power might mix with mine and the ley line I now had simmering under my skin was another issue altogether, but it was a cross-that-bridge-when-we-get-there kind of question.

All this tumbled around in my head as Zeus shook in the middle of the sigil, pain clear on his once-smug face. I refocused all my intention on smelling and tasting, teasing out all the individual ingredients of the mingled magic pulsing through the sigil to then call all of it back to me. The tastes came, the earthiness of the ley power with my own darkness and Zeus's ozone. Each thread was a bright bite on my tongue. I concentrated, pulling each thread into my mind. Soon, I began to gulp down power.

It was a torrent. I felt like I was drowning for a moment, magic cramming itself down my throat, filling my lungs, and making it hard to breathe. It unfurled inside me when it hit my gut, seeking every nook and cranny, twisting in separate, searing sparks all around my insides, and pulsing so hard and filling me so completely, I got lost in the overriding energy and force of three distinct and massive types of power. The magic was taking over, forcing what was me into a small ball at the back of my mind, and there wasn't anything I could do to stop it.

I didn't really want to stop it because the magic rode me hard and started calling me to its wild will inside of me. My eyes clouded in a dark haze, and a blink later I saw sparkling darkness, crisper and clearer than my everyday vision, my eyes now honed by multiple godly and earthly magics running riot in my human form. I was me somewhere inside, but also, I wasn't. The magic recognized itself in a human form, not as human and not as me but something it could break loose from, something it could transcend. Something it could shed in order to become a dark, glittering beacon of power.

I registered a cry, and the magic turned my head back toward Zeus. He was withered and shaking, a near husk of his former self. Vicious will rose inside me, directing my hand and forcing me to take in his power more quickly, until I drained every last drop, and he was nothing but a body of a once-god, still trapped. Forever powerless.

I let him down and he lay clutching grass in his grasping hands. My skin crackled with raw magical power. I heard words, maybe a cry or two, but my focus was all on Zeus. I walked up, my feet sparking with white-hot lightning with each step I took. There was no need to try to break the sigil; the mass of magic coming down with my foot was enough for the crack to sound and I stalked toward the defeated Other God. I felt nothing but need and power in the moment as I looked at him shivering in the warm grass.

"I have seen such before, will see such again. You, however, will not." It was a distant observation of reality. Not a threat but fact. As I spoke it, what was supposed to be my voice held the same echo Ny's sometimes took on, but it sounded more hollow to the tiny part of me now banging around in my head to take back over. It couldn't though. The crush of magic inside was in the driver's seat, and it did what it wished, ignoring my personal thoughts and needs.

My sparking black vision saw nothing from him, only a body needing to be destroyed, so my body did what the magic willed. Raising a hand, I sent out Zeus's lightning, mixed with the added power of the ley line magic and my shadow magic. There was no lingering burn, no crumbling to ash. It was a nuclear detonation. One second, Zeus was shivering and broken on the ground. The next, a scorched circle marked the earth and the smell of burnt flesh lingered in the air. He was gone, fully destroyed. Never to return again because his power now coursed through my body.

I didn't rejoice or anything. I was still struggling to get back control because the power was all there was. I felt DD tremble down the line as it zipped over to check on me. My black eyes studied it for a moment before the magic swatted it away, pushing it to the ground with a hard crackling snap. A gasp went up and the power whipped my head around. I heard something like a growl from my own throat, my lips forming a harsh snarl before a tinge of pain laced over it from the lingering effects of Zeus's fists. My hand moved up, spark and shadow mixed in a quick burst, and my face healed with a small touch of power, the magic making its vessel whole and pain-free once again.

"Randy?" Harley asked. Of course she knew I wasn't in control anymore. I couldn't answer her, and the magic was distracted by the power now stepping beside her: Mia, the Necronomicon in the flesh, magic stored in another body and ready to be used. My power couldn't have that, so it flung out and caged the two women as I stalked forward, spear held high.

Rich tackled me to the ground, his ghoul speed intercepting me before the power made my body strike a blow I could never forgive. He snapped at my neck with his powerful jaw and teeth, but I easily pushed him off me, the lightning flashing across my skin, drawing a hard yelp from him as he was thrown off my body.

My body stood in a graceful leap, only concerned with the women the magic saw as threats in front of me. Luckily, Gareth was still there. He grabbed hold from behind, DD a tiny shield over his skin so the lightning crackle of my new power couldn't penetrate right away. What did penetrate me—what made my mind and being, the Randy part of me, stronger—was the Gareth calm I'd come to know. The sense of connection and rightness I'd always felt with him somehow pushed through all the power and bolstered me inside all of it.

Then a different darkness, more complete and encompassing, fell across my vision. It was Ny, holding his book and strolling toward me with his loose-hipped walk, his face determined and hard. The magic's focus immediately shifted from the women I'd caged to him. The Outer God was the biggest threat now, his power on par with what raged inside my body. Another growl, a gnash of teeth at the Prince, even as I tried to push the power aside and take the reins again.

Ny stopped a breath away from me, his head moving in the feline way of his as he studied my face. "This is not you, sweetling."

I knew that, but the magic didn't, and it was still screaming for a fight. It was also literally screaming at Ny, right in his beautiful sandy-brown face, so hard and harsh it ruffled the flopping bits of his thick black hair.

"Harness it," he said, his starry gaze locking with mine, his will shining through even though he wasn't using his power on me. "Get control, Randy. Center yourself, not this power."

He was right, of course. Intention, control. Those were the keys to all magic, even magic this big. I'd been built to handle the magic of a goddess; what was a little more thrown on top of it? The thing was I had a hard time centering when the power in me was struggling with all its might to take out the magic it saw as a threat, which just happened to be all the people I loved gathered around.

Distantly I heard a familiar ring, one I had almost forgotten could sound in my head. When the shrill cry of a telephone echoed in my mind, the part of me that was still me raced toward it, seeing a simple headset with a curly line hovering in blank space in my head as power and energy in blue, black, and stark white swirled around it, testing it.

"Merry, stay away!" I screamed as I held the phone to my ear. "Don't you fucking come here."

Her voice sounded distant, like she was speaking through a tunnel, when she said, "Randy, I love you. Stay safe. You can do this! You. You hear me!"

An old-school beeping disconnect sounded. I stared at the phone in my imaginary hand deep in my own head, and I conjured memories. Of Merry, Mia, and me as children, running and playing and laughing and fighting. Loving. Harley as we trained together, as we plotted and planned. The hard, muscled bulk of Gareth and the lean lines of Ny, how each felt different but also so similar. All these people close, all these people I loved, now in danger because I apparently couldn't get my shit together.

I could do this. Me. Like Merry said. Because I was the one in control, or at least the one who should be in control. Others' actions, others' magics, and others' decisions had devasted my small world. The big world too. I'd come along and right some of it. Me. With all my human messiness, packed alongside my godly power. The magic had chosen me, and whether I understood the choice or not, it'd proven right again and again in these past few months. It was time for me to start making my own moves, literally and figuratively wresting control back for myself.

The worry, the fear, all the masses of guilt... Well, they didn't disappear instantly with this well of new self-determination. They did ease up some as I realized control wasn't about wrestling every little thing around me into submission but letting what I knew guide what I did, for better or worse—as all the other good and shitty gods and mages and people I knew did.

I stopped struggling in my mind, went back to basics, and focused all that was me on the intention of control, of being me again—if not for myself, then in order to protect all these people I cared about who were trying to bring me back to me. I shook my head, the first physical action I consciously did, and the power bucked inside, forcing my body to roll between Ny and Gareth. The contact of the two, the memory of all our contact, the love there, helped center me even more. It helped me force the magic down and focus in on the thrum and beat I'd always known, the place where my magic resided in me and as a part of me, but never in control of me. Because magic and I were one, even this new doubled-up godly power, but I was Randy Carter, damnit, and I was in control of myself.

I forced my dark eyes closed, imagined my Warm Regards kitchen, my happy place from meditation, and saw the tasting threads of all this magic laid out on one of my stainless-steel prep tables like long strips of dough. One was blue, one black, and one bright white, all twisting and turning, living things fighting for dominance against each other. I began to braid, making a massive loaf by weaving each strip together with the others, forming a whole. When it was done, my hands feeling the ache of forcing power to my will, I stepped back and saw it merge and become something together with me, all the power and my consciousness in flash.

My body shuddered. I blinked my eyes open and looked into Ny's concerned gaze. "Ny?" I whispered.

His lids fell and rose again, his chest heaving in a stiff staccato beat, and a tear hovered right at the corner of his spacey gaze. He hugged me tight from the front as I heard Gareth whisper, "Randy. Oh, shit, Randy," behind me, his calm embrace causing me to sag back into him so I could feel his solidness behind me as I took Ny's weight in front of me.

DD zipped up, trembling as it stroked down my cheek. "Sorry, buddy," I croaked out between tears. It ignored the apology but stayed close, warmth and relief reaching me down our line.

Ny stepped back, taking my shoulders in his hands as he studied my face. "My sweetling," he said, awe in his eyes and voice. "You wrangled an incredible amount of power."

"More like kneaded it, but it's done. All braided up tight in here," I said as I snaked a hand between our bodies and patted my gut.

"Move!" Mia yelled as she shoved the Outer God out of her way.

His head whipped around abnormally fast, and Rich might have moved just as quickly to get between the two if need be, but Ny simply did as she asked, letting Mia slam into my front. Gareth also let go.

"I'm so, so sorry," I said to Mia, then tracked Harley to include her, tears spilling freely down my face in a steady stream.

"No need to apologize. If anyone knows what it's like to have something work in you, it's me, sis. I get it. No harm, no foul."

I swallowed down the guilt, because she was right. I hadn't done it. It wasn't me who'd caused the problem, but I'd been the one to take over and fix it. The relief of knowing I could and would take on only what I'd done myself in the future caused my chest to twinge in a good way.

I felt Harley's hand at my right shoulder, and she gave it a squeeze before another hit pushed her into me and familiar arms wrapped around all of us. Merry had clearly ignored my warning about not showing up and was now crying big old happy tears as her hands moved over Harley and me and Mia, never stopping for long on one of us before checking the next was whole and there.

WE ALL ENDED UP back at Ny's place because it was closer and most of us couldn't shadow walk. There were tears, a bit of rehashing, and maybe some gallows humor thrown around. Merry's twisting, nervous hands calmed eventually, with some holding from Harley. Mia's body seemed more relaxed than I'd seen it in months, something in her now connected and at peace with what was hanging around inside her head. Rich curling her into his big arms on Ny's couch also probably helped. I sat at the table sandwiched between my guys, their chairs pulled close and their arms thrown over me.

Ny's power sizzled hard across my skin, but not in an uncomfortable way. He was on par with what I'd always felt around Azathoth, though not quite there. He'd tucked the Book of Knowing away somewhere, after using it to connect to his missing power, and now was full-on Nyarlathotep once again. I couldn't be fully sure there was a big difference, or any difference in him, beyond power level. Same lounging coolness, same studying and sardonic gaze, same sexy smirk. Just a lot more oomph behind it. No one else acted concerned about it, and I didn't feel concerned or anything, so I figured it was what it was. Ny was a whole-ass Outer God now, but he was still my Ny, my Prince, and I was glad as hell for it.

After we were done chatting, when exhaustion finally won out over the fear something else would pop up, people started filtering out. First Mia and Rich headed home after some big hugs and a whispered thanks from me to Rich for what he'd done to stop not-really-me from hurting Mia and Harley. Soon after they left, Harley and Merry went to go, after a crushing hug from my sister and a wide smile from Harley.

"More training now?" she asked before they hit the door.

I groaned. "For the love of the gods, woman, give me a break!"

Harley laughed, gave a nod to the three of us hovering by the door, and exited as she guided a waving, smiling Merry out with a firm hand at the small of her back.

The door shut and I sagged, sandwiched still between Ny and Gareth. I let them take my weight, needing it. Needing closeness. "Thank you," I said, not looking up.

"No need to thank us, Randy," Gareth grumbled before planting a kiss on the top of my head.

Ny gave my waist a squeeze and said, "We'd come for you any time, sweetling."

I knew they would, which was why the new magic in my gut wasn't scaring the shit out of me right then. Maybe one day it would, but not then, when I was plastered between the two guys I loved. Because it was love and care and memory that had brought me back to me, grounded me, and I knew I'd always have it at my fingertips, whenever and wherever I needed it.

I was happy things were resolved, or at least the whole "Zeus-overthrow plot threatening the people I loved and most of the wider human world" was now done. I was also hella worn out, so all I did was smile from one to the other and said, "Let's go to bed," before I took each in hand and guided them toward the stairs. They followed, without reservation, as I knew they always would.

# Epilogue

I STOOD STARING AT a prep table in the middle of the kitchen at Warm Regards. It was a replica of the table from my Franklin Park vision weeks ago, but this was real. Placed there after the contractor's crew finished all the repairs. Everything was exactly the same, all shiny and newly repaired. Correction. Everything but the color was the same. They'd repainted the walls a bluish gray that leaned more toward navy. It was much darker than the buttery yellow from before, but the darker tone felt fitting. For me and the space.

It was several weeks after the big final showdown, and Ohio was firmly in fall territory. Nate had helped me bake and prep a number of tasty treats, many featuring pumpkin or maple, the day before. He was out front, chatting with the counter workers as we finished final prep for our grand reopening.

I was alone in the kitchen, thinking back to so much that had happened. Deb had been killed here, and it would always pain me to think of it. I'd also had my first conversations with Harley and Gareth here. I'd met Ny in his human form in this building. I'd had countless laughs with Merry and Mia here. Lots of pain and horror but also so much damn good. Kind of like my life now—a shit show calmed and cooled.

After walking to the spot where Deb had been broken, I crouched and took a deep cleansing breath. The guilt had eased since I'd taken out Zeus and came out master of my own powers. I'd learned to place blame where it needed to be placed and let go of the things I couldn't control or change. Didn't mean I didn't still feel grief and sadness. Didn't mean I would ever forget. Just meant I wouldn't tear myself apart over it anymore, because what had happened to her wasn't on me. It was on some assholes who were now no more. "I'm so, so sorry, Deb," I whispered to no one and kissed my hand before placing it on the floor. I'd probably do this again, many times, but this one was important. Sad and freeing all at once.

"Randy?" Nate called from the doorway, and I looked up and saw him frown down at me on the ground. He walked over and helped me to my feet. "Gareth texted. They're all going to be here soon, before the doors open. It was supposed to be a surprise, but…" He didn't finish, and I got the uncertainty. He wanted me prepared today because he knew, just as Mia knew, the memory of what had gone down here could rear back at any time.

"It's fine," I said before standing and looping my elbow through his. "We got this. First, let me wash my hands. Don't need floor germs in our baking." My shadows twirled around Nate a moment, sparks of blue and white now speckling the shade. DD bounced around Nate's head, and he smiled its way, now able to see it after more mage training. DD was always happy here, or anywhere it was with the people it cared about in this realm. Very much like me.

Nate chuckled at my words and the hovering antics of DD. It was small but lifting because it was so good to hear laughter in this space again. It made everything feel whole, complete. Finished but ready for whatever the future might hold.

Please take a moment to rate *Shadow of the Other Gods* on Amazon.
Every rating/review helps!
Stay up to date with all things Sonya Lawson at sonyalawson.com.

# WANT MORE?

Want to read a free prequel novella all about Randy, Merry, and Mia? Download *Shadow in the Storm* on Bookfunnel (https://BookHip.com/TCWWJGT), free with a newsletter sign up.

Interested in what Nyarlathotep was up to before he walked into Randy's life? Join my newsletter and get a free (& very steamy) prequel story featuring the Prince of the Dreamlands via BookFunnel (https://BookHip.com/HNSGPTJ).

Want to read other books by Sonya Lawson? You can find her book pages below:

The Comus Duology

In Dreams of Dragons

# Acknowledgements

Because this is an end of sorts, things are a little long here. It just means my life is so full I have to take a lot of space to thank everyone who should be thanked, which is a good thing for me. So here it is.

Novel Nurse Editing has edited every piece of Randy Carter fiction, from the early stories to the prequel and through all four novels. It's often hard to find editors as an indie writer, so I'm eternally grateful I found Janna and Angie so early on in my indie author career. Their advice, care, and attention to detail are all top notch. I can't recommend them highly enough, and I hope we have a very long future together with many more words to come.

100 Covers again did this amazing cover and I have nothing but praise for their dedication and talent for making Randy come to life in various ways. I must admit, this one is my favorite of the bunch, so a special thanks for helping my series go out with a bank.

Every day I am thankful I went to a particular Mexican restaurant in Vegas on a particular night of a writer's conference. It was there I (mostly) met and bonded with A.R., B.Z., Karri, Kassie, Kenzie, and Nicole. They're MBs and my writing rocks. I couldn't imagine a more spectacular group of strong, thoughtful, caring, supportive, and damn funny writers and friends. Your help with craft, business, and the everyday messes of life have helped me across every writerly hurdle, and I truly love you all.

My Wednesday Mastermind group – including, at various times, Gary, Jamie, Kat, Marie, Olivia, and Scott – are the best sounding boards for an indie author. We're all different, and write very different genres and styles, but our differences make our group so effective and helpful. A different set of eyes is sometimes all you need to make progress. Thank you all for the advice and encouragement along the way.

My CBs – Andy, Bonnie, Jose, and Kyle – gave me a much-needed break when I was in the middle of edits. As always, it was fun times. They're family by bond, much like most of the characters in Randy carter's life, so thanks for the love and constant inspiration.

Big shout out to Lynn, another sister by bond if not blood, for showing me so much awesomeness in Columbus over the years and for always asking me how my writing is going whenever we speak.

My dad is always asking about my books. He even considers out of the box advertising ideas (such as trying to make indie book billboards a thing). More than this, he's forever supported and loved me, and never missed an opportunity to say he's proud of me.

My older brother, Shannon, also deserves to be included because he's all about the support, even shilling my books for me to his own fans (on his paranormal investigation page).

To be honest, none of this would be possible without the unwavering support of my husband. Ario helps with the logistics, the marketing, and production. He lets me bounce ideas off him. More than anything, though, he encourages me to pursue my dreams in any form they take. He's the best, truly, and no Randy story would exist without him.

Finally, and once more, I have to thank all my beautiful readers out there. You make my heart feel big. I'm so happy I could share Randy with you – and that you came to care about her, too. Truly, deeply – thank you.

# About the Author

Sonya Lawson is a recovering academic currently writing steamy modern fantasy with maybe a few too many literary references. Her stories may differ, but they all have at least one common characteristic — sassy, intelligent women trying to do the best they can in whatever world they inhabit.

While she remains a rural Kentuckian at heart, she's spent a lot of time in the Midwest and currently lives in the Pacific Northwest. She fills her days with writing, editing, reading, walking through old forests, and watching sitcoms or horror films with her husband. Two rowdy cats terrorize her house regularly, but she loves it.

You can find more information about past books, current projects, and upcoming releases at www.sonyalawson.com.

Don't forget to follow her on all her socials to stay connected. Find her on TikTok, Instagram, and Facebook using her username @sonyalawsonwrites.